ANN KELLEY is a photographer and r-
ly played cricket for Cornwall. She   c-
tion of poems and photographs, a   es
and an audio book of cat stories. She lives with her second husband
and several cats on the edge of a cliff in Cornwall where they have
survived a flood, a landslip, a lightning strike and the roof blowing
off. She runs courses for aspiring poets at her home, writing courses
for medics and medical students, and speaks about her poetry therapy
work with patients at medical conferences.

Inchworm

ANN KELLEY

Luath Press Limited

EDINBURGH

www.luath.co.uk

First published 2008

ISBN (10): 1-906307-62-8
ISBN (13): 978-1-906307-62-2

The paper used in this book is recyclable.
It is made from low chlorine pulps
produced in a low energy, low emission manner
from renewable forests.

Printed and bound by Norhaven A/S, Viborg, Denmark

Typeset in 11 point Sabon

Many thanks to Bella, Simon, Sonny, Eiofe and Jake Hassett, Dr Kate Dalziel, Lisa Innes, Alan Naftalin, and Chloe Flora Foreman for inspiration, ideas and advice. And all friends and family who made suggestions and let me steal words out of their mouths.

To all organ donors and their families.
Thank you for the gift of hope.

PROLOGUE

The unexamined life is a life not worth living – SOCRATES

ALISTAIR SWERVES TO miss a huge heap of something in the middle of the road. It's 3 a.m., the dead of night, the end of the year.

'What the...?'

Mum stirs in the front passenger seat. 'There's another.'

'What is it?'

'Looks like elephant shit,' I say.

Alistair winds down the window. Mum says, 'Smells like elephant shit.'

Around the bend we come across them. Trunk to tail, the troupe tiptoe silently through the sleeping London street.

'A circus?'

'It's lucky to see elephants,' I say. I need all the luck I can get. I am on my way to have a heart and lung transplant.

CHAPTER ONE

Intensive Therapy Unit

MY FIRST THOUGHTS on waking are – Where are my cats? I feel no pain but I do have tubes coming out of every orifice, plus one or two new holes in my chest and other places. My throat is sore and I can't talk. Mummy is here wearing a hospital gown and surgical mask, though I can still see her tears, and Daddy looks anxiously through the glass door. He can't come in because he has bugs up his nose.

It's several days since the transplant. I am pretty drugged up and sleep a lot but everything went well, according to my cardiac surgeon. I have lots of nurses. Someone watches me all the time. It's like having slaves. They turn me, wash me, change my dressings, take my temperature and blood pressure about a million times a day. There are machines all around me, monitoring all my bodily functions. I have catheters and bags of liquids going in and out of me, but I am now breathing without mechanical assistance. Various drugs are being fed into my veins. I feel sleepy but contented, not worried. The physiotherapist comes to make me cough. She calls me Gorgeous Gussie. She makes me laugh and it hurts.

Daddy strokes my hand. His nose germs have gone. There's a canula taped onto the back of my hand. He keeps forgetting and knocking it. It stings. I glare at him and he apologises.

Thoughts flutter in my head and out again like a flock of

pigeons rising from earth in a panicked bunch, like tickertape: loose sheets of paper snatched by the breeze.

Alistair cannot come into the Intensive Therapy unit, even though he's a doctor, because he isn't related. He waves through the window at me, blows kisses and gives the thumbs up sign.

I sleep and I am in a ball of pain. I am everyone who has lived, who is living now, who is going to live, and we are all in pain and this ball of pain is God. I am God. And the pain is everlasting. But with all my strength and power I force the pain into millions of parts, millions of people sharing the ball of pain, and I force the pain into a flat line of time – past, present and future. I am God, and God is everyone, and we all share the pain.

I open my eyes and see nurses, my invention, sharing my pain.

Was it a nightmare? It seems too real; I am still God, I am still in pain, but the pain is less, fading. There is a dreadful stench, like a dead elephant. I dare not close my eyes because I am terrified. It's then that I remember, I've had this dream before. It is only a dream.

Room 3, B Ward

When I can talk again, I ask my nurse, Katy, if she is real. She laughs.

'I was last time I looked,' she says.

'Is there a horrid smell?'

She sniffs. 'No more than usual,' She is doing something to my IV line. I suddenly start to cry.

4

'Gussie, what is it, darling?'

'I had a nasty dream. It was awful. And I…'

I'm afraid I blubber.

'Nightmares are common after transplant, I'm afraid. Lots of people get them. You mustn't worry, they'll go away.'

I ask for a mirror. My chest is covered in a wide tape, so I can't see the clips or incision but I want to see my face, to see if I've changed.

I have – I'm pink! Pink cheeks! Pink lips! Normal coloured. Not blue any more. I look normal. I don't know whose heart and lungs I have inherited. It feels weird, very weird: not quite a robot but someone else's heart and lungs working inside me, attached to my veins and arteries. Like putting a new engine in a clapped-out car. I was clapped-out, breathless all the time, fainting, and my heart racing like a steam train going through a tunnel. Chest pains, palpitations, nausea, dizziness, exhaustion, headaches, cyanosis, the usual stuff. I can't wait to try out my new motor. Will I have the donor's memories or habits? Perhaps I'll start scratching my bum or tapping my foot. I could blame all my bad habits on my donor! Perhaps I will suddenly crave Brussels sprouts or black olives, perhaps I'll be able to speak Russian or be mad on motor racing or Manchester United? If my donor was unhappy, will I have her bad memories? I hope she wasn't allergic to cats; what a terrible thought. At pre-op meetings I was told that I wouldn't acquire any of a donor's traits. The heart is a pump and the lungs are bellows: they don't carry memory. It's a myth, they said. I won't suddenly be an expert on quantum mechanics. Shame.

I don't feel like a different person. My eyes look the same. It's the same old Gussie staring out of them. Maybe I look a little older. I might start growing now, growing tits and hips and pubic hair. Getting taller. Putting on weight.

'If I asked the doctors, do you think I could see my old heart and lungs, Mum?'

'You gruesome little beast, no, I shouldn't think so.'

'Oh, why not?' It would be fascinating to see my old organs, to see the disease I was born with. I hope they are going to keep them to show medical students.

'Let's concentrate on looking after the new organs, shall we?' says one of the nurses, Katy, who has just done a blood test and is now is doing something to my IV lines.

I have the same hallucination as I had before. It's so scary. I hate it. I'm having an anti-psychosis drug to make the horrors go away.

Mum brings in some music for me, with ear phones. I don't know what it is, but Alistair sent it. It's Handel's Arias for opera or something, very soothing. He said to listen to it when I go to sleep and then the horrors won't come back.

I sleep and dream I'm running along Porthmeor Beach, with my cats following me. The sky is pink and the sea flat. Suddenly an elephant appears, swimming majestically, then another and another. They form a circle and raise their trumpets and squirt water into the sky, like an illustration in a Babar story. I wake feeling wonderful, sore but happy. I can breathe, fill my new lungs; soon I'll be able to run along the beach again.

I can't wait to go home to my cats, my darling Charlie and bossy Flo and scaredy-cat Rambo. To see Brett and my new family: Claire and Moss, Gabriel, Troy and Phaedra, and Fay, my great Aunt Fay. I'll be able to go to school. I am so grateful to my donor and his/her family. Without them I would not be alive. And suddenly I am in tears for that dead person and her grieving family and friends.

It rains every day but I love the raindrops running down the hospital window, the blurred bones of leafless trees. I love the starlings waddling across the grey grass; a robin's red breast the only colour in the January landscape, like a still from *Doctor Zhivago*, the sky a khaki grey-green; I'm growing fond of the muffled sound of a helicopter landing with someone arriving for a transplant, or maybe the transplant coordinator delivering an icebox with organs in.

Today's biopsy shows no signs of rejection, no inflammation.

My first walk: I'm helped, of course, but to be vertical and walking is marvellous. I don't feel as breathless as I did BT (Before Transplant). A whole load of tubes, like a milking machine, accompanies me. The cardiac monitor has been unplugged, so I can move about but I feel woozy and have to get back to my bed, my safe island.

Later I find myself talking to my new heart and lungs as if they are visitors and I want them to feel at home. In fact they are more like adopted children, who will settle down and learn to love me as I learn to live with them, hopefully. Otherwise – disaster! 'Now I hope you don't miss your other body too much, though I'm sure you will for a while, until you get used to being inside me. I promise to look after you. I'll do plenty of exercise and have my teeth checked regularly so I don't get infections. I'll eat all the right foods and never eat smoked salmon or unpasteurised cheese.' (I will have to avoid food poisoning as I am immunosuppressed owing to all the antibiotics etc that I have to take. At the moment I am pumped full of painkillers, Septrin, cyclosporine, all sorts of drugs with long names.)

'I can't take you to a foreign country for a year,' I tell my new organs. 'I can't remember why, but that's all right because we're going to live in Cornwall, and that's like a foreign country. It's got banana trees and palm trees.' I press my hand against my chest and say, 'I promise you you'll love it. I'll never eat shellfish or blue cheese or rare meat. And no soft eggs.'

Bloody hell, am I going to have to survive on vegetable soup?

If the heart cannot feel why do we say heartfelt? Deep in my heart? Heart throb? Heartache? Heartbroken? Fainthearted? Eat your heart out? Lose my heart to...? Set my heart on doing something? Braveheart? With all my heart? (I am told that because of some surgical procedure I will feel no pain from my new heart, so no heartache then.)

I've asked Daddy to lend me a camera – I left mine in Cornwall – so I can record what goes on here in hospital. He gives me one of his own precious cameras – an old Leica. It's fiddly to load the film but it's smaller than my Nikkormat and not as heavy. It has to be sprayed with disinfectant before I can use it. Hope it doesn't harm the works. I make portraits of all the nurses and doctors who come into the room, the cleaner, the physio, my pale-blue room, the machines behind my bed, the view through the window, and Mum. Mum has lots of grey hairs. Shall I tell her? She looks older and anxious, but she's always looked anxious.

I'm not allowed out of my room yet. It's like being in prison. But I have mail!

Der Gussie,
How ar yu? I am good. My rabits and duks are good.
My cats are good. Zennor is good. She et wun ov

*Claire's best shoos. I hope you will get beeter and I
will sea yu sooon.
Luv,
Gabriel xx*

(He has drawn a picture of his puppy chewing a shoe. It was
in the same envelope as Fay's Get Well Soon card that had a
lovely drawing of a tabby cat on it by an artist called Gwen
John.)

*My dearest Gussie,
I hear you are doing very well and making a good
recovery. It will be lovely to see you again – my little
great niece! We will have great times when you come
home. Do you like the ballet? I can take you if you
like, with Phaedra (if she's not surfing). There's a
good Dutch dance company performing in Truro in
the spring. Hopefully you will be back by then. My
naughty cat Six-toes killed one of the chicks – the
black one. She is banished from the garden now and
has to stay indoors. She is very cross as you may
imagine.
Get well quickly, my brave little darling, we are all
thinking of you,
Lots of love,
Fay xxx*
PS *Claire, Moss, Phaedra and Troy all send love and
kisses.*

They had all put messages on the card:

*Masses of love, thinking of you, Claire and all the
Darlings. xxx*

Be good, love Phaedra. xxxxxxxxx

YAY GUSSIE!!! – Troy x

Looking forward to seeing you soon, lots of love, Moss. xxx

On a home-made card covered in stuck-on silver stars and pink hearts:

Dear Gussie,
I hope you are feeling better. I can't wait to see you again. When are you coming home to Cornwall?
SCHOOL IS HORRIBLE. MY SISTER IS HORRIBLE. I am feeling dark night blue without you.
Can't wait to see your scar, is it brill?
Love, Bridget xxxxxxx

(Bridget lives in colour, thinks and feels in colour. Not like ordinary people who see red, feel blue, are yellow-bellied. She has an existence made up of an artist's palette of vivid colours. A weird and interesting child with a purple pain in the neck of a sister, Siobhan, who has her eye on Brett, and anything in trousers.)

Bridget has put a small gold paper star inside the envelope in a separate folded up piece of tissue. When I unfold the tissue there's a message that says:

To my gold star best friend Gussie. xxxxxxxxxx

A card with a print of a Matisse bluebird paper cut-out:

Howyadoin Guss?

*It's cold here and there's lots of rain so we haven't
been birding lately and I can't use the big telescope.
Buddy has flown. He came back once or twice to
visit. Made loads of racket so's I'd go out and see
him, but I think he's truly independent now. Probably
joined the large flock up the road. Will you be able to
start school when you come back?
Hope you're not feeling too crook.
Miss you Guss,
Brett x*

On the back of a picture postcard showing the harbour,
St Ives:

*Dear Gussie,
Forgive my poor handwriting. It is because I cannot
see very well.
You will be happy to hear that Charlie, Flo and
Rambo are all eating well and not moping too much
without you. They are getting on quite well with my
Shandy, so don't you worry about them. I am having
my eye op soon and the cats will go to the Darlings
until you come home.
That's all for now dear, but I hope you are getting on
well and I'll see you soon,
Love,
Mrs Thomas*

It's strange seeing Daddy after all this time. He looks thinner
than I remember and he's going grey at the front and sides.
He's more handsome than ever, even with his chin all bristly.
I make a photo of him, finishing the roll of film.

'My best side,' he insists. He brought a huge bunch of red

roses but wasn't allowed to give them to me. Flowers aren't allowed, or cards. Germs. Mum has to read my cards, then take them away.

Daddy has taken my film to be processed.

Alistair has to go back to Cornwall to work soon, but Mummy will stay in a hospital flat to be close to me. Daddy said she could stay in his flat but she declined. I don't think he has a girlfriend at the moment, or not one he's mentioned anyway, but Mum says she'd rather be here so she can be close to me. He's off on one of his business trips soon and so we can stay at his place for at least a couple of weeks when I get out of hospital. We have to stay near the hospital for three months so the doctors can check on my progress, make sure I don't reject the organs, and ensure the drugs are working. There are lots of drugs to take, five times a day at first. If you shook me I'd rattle. I'm going to have to be very careful to take them at the same time each day. Mum will take charge of my medicines and has a chart so she can tick them off as I swallow them. My scar is sore, of course, and it will take about a year before it fades. Maybe by the time I've grown breasts and can wear a bikini on the beach it won't be so bad. Or maybe I'll start a fashion of wearing loads of clothes on the beach, hiding my body completely, The Mystery Girl. Actually, if I wore a one-piece swimsuit you couldn't see the scar at all. Anyway, I like scars: they're like badges of honour or medals showing how brave you've been, and how experienced in the knocks life gives you.

There's a quote from someone in one of the hospital leaflets that says about a transplant patient, '*You have traded death for a lifetime of medical management.*'

I am allowed to have a bath today. I can't believe how easy it is to breathe. It makes me realise how ill I felt before the operation. I do exercises to strengthen my heart muscle. I hold up my hands and admire my newly pink fingernails. So lovely! Maybe I'll stop biting them now. Pink – my favourite colour.

But the best thing is feeling energetic. I can't believe how well I feel.

There was a little boy on ICU – Jordan, he was six – but I didn't get to know him. His operation wasn't successful; there were complications and he died last night. The nurses were crying.

There was also a boy of about fourteen, Precious. What an unusual, beautiful name! He's too hunky to have a name like Precious. It's no stranger than Bonny, River, Sky or Summer, though, or Hope, Joy or Faith. He had his transplant (heart only) the day after me so he is in a similar state of recovery. We see each other most days in physiotherapy sessions and clinics and support group meetings.

He is from Zimbabwe and his mother is staying in a hospital flat. Precious speaks excellent English in a soft whispering voice. He was born healthy but developed life-threatening heart problems last year and needed a transplant to survive. He has some family in England luckily and was able to wait here for his donor heart. His skin is the colour of treacle toffee and he has a wide-open face and smile. He is a good runner, or used to be, he tells me, and hopes to be again.

I have offered to teach him to play Scrabble. Mum is delighted that I have found a friend. It takes the pressure off her. She spends a lot of time talking to Agnes, his mother. She told my mum that his father, a doctor, is still in Zimbabwe with their two daughters and she worries about them because there are food and fuel shortages there and the people are rioting.

I sleep and dream I am unable to walk or run; I am in a wheelchair, strapped in and cannot move. I cannot breathe. I wake sobbing, relieved.

My cardiac surgeon, Mr Sami is very good looking. He's Egyptian and is like a Pharaoh, with a hooked nose like my cat Charlie, dark eyes and thick lashes. Mum thinks he's hunky and she practically salivates whenever he visits me. He's pleased with my progress.

'My star patient', he calls me. I bet he says that to all his patients. There's usually about six other doctors with him but I don't know their names.

My fingers and fingernails look normal – not clubbed any more and no longer blue. I'm pink all over!

Mummy reads to me each day from *The House at Pooh Corner,* which is the book I chose to bring with me to hospital, or tells me stories about when I was little or when she was a child. It is one of the compensations of being post-operative. I can't get enough of it: being read to is my favourite thing in the world. Mum is particularly good at it – reading out loud. She does the voices and really gets into the heart of it. She also likes Winnie the Pooh even though we both know most of the stories off by heart. By heart – what a strange expression. Will my new heart be a good learner?

She's reading me the first story where Winnie the Pooh is trying to look like a small black cloud to fool the bees, and he rolls in mud and then uses a blue balloon to float up as high as the honeycomb. Oh, you have to read it.

CHAPTER TWO

A WEEK AGO I woke with a high temperature, palpitations, swollen ankles and legs and felt very breathless and as if I had flu. I was having acute rejection. I was put on a different drug regime and given an IV line into my arm. I spent the week feeling awful and having loads of tests – biopsies, ECG (electrocardiogram) and echocardiogram (an ultrasound picture of the heart) and blood tests. I'm better now, but feel rather weak and tearful. Also, the intravenous steroids have made me look like a hamster, with huge round cheeks.

Soo Yong helps me to a drink of water and makes me more comfortable.

'Khob Koon,' I conjure the words for thank you from my winter in Thailand years ago. She is so pleased. I wish I knew more foreign words; there are many nurses and doctors here from other countries.

I keep thinking about the person who died so I could live. I know he or she didn't actually die so that I can live, but that's what it feels like. I feel almost like I wanted her to die so I could use her heart and lungs. That's a dreadful feeling. Do I miss my old organs? No, I don't think so, except that I knew the noises my old heart and lungs made inside my chest, the thumping and wheezing and erratic heart beat like an express train going through a tunnel. Now, I am aware all the time of these strange organs and I really can't tell if the odd feelings I get are a result of the trauma of the operation or are they signs of something not being right? Katy reassures me that all is now well and I mustn't worry. This is just a blip and they will adjust my medication until they get it right. In the hospital folder we were given that tells all about transplantation of organs, *chronic* rejection is the worst thing that can happen. The arteries become blocked and then you get heart failure. I'll have to have regular tests to make sure that isn't happening for one to three years post transplant.

> The most common causes of death following a transplant are infection or rejection of the heart. Patients on drugs to prevent rejection are at risk of side effects: developing kidney damage, high blood pressure, osteoporosis (thinning of the bones) and lymphoma (a type of cancer that affects cells of the immune system). Coronary artery disease and bronchiolitis (in which there are obstructions in the airways of the lungs) are a problem too.

All this I learn from transplant information leaflets.

So, anyway, I'm probably not in for an easy ride – more of a ride on a mad elephant who might throw me down and trample on me. I think of my immune system cells as burly bouncers who stalk around looking for gatecrashers, uninvited guests at a party. When they see my strange new heart and lungs, they desperately try to eject them from my body. I must take the immunosuppressants – drugs that suppress the immune system so the new organs are not damaged. Never must I forget to take the drugs, even if they bring me other new problems. Hopefully those problems can be cured by yet more drugs.

There's a big, black bird, some sort of crow, in the tree outside my window, hunched and ugly, peering in at me.

'Close the curtains, Mum.'

'Why, darling, are your eyes hurting?'

'No, just close them.'

'Please?'

'Please.'

CHAPTER THREE

NEGLECT—TO TREAT CARELESSLY; TO FAIL TO BESTOW DUE CARE UPON

NOSTALGIA—HOMESICKNESS; SENTIMENTAL LONGING FOR PAST TIMES

MUM HAS A dictionary that we use for Scrabble when we need to look up the correct spelling of a word or when we're not sure if a word exists. I'm resuming my self-education. I am choosing one or two new words to use each day. I used to do that BT. It's a good way of learning stuff that I have missed out on by not going to school. My education has been sadly neglected. Mum says there have been other more important things to think about – like keeping me alive. I am *Girl, Interrupted* (a new game – naming people after movies). Brett's mum was my home tutor for a short time before I came into hospital. Maybe I could still have her if I can't go back to school straight away when we go back to Cornwall?

Precious is so much more active than me. He is doing well in physio. I expect that's because he was fitter before he became seriously ill, if that makes sense. And he hasn't had any problems since his transplant. I haven't yet thought of a film name for him. He's a difficult one. *The African Queen* is out. He's definitely too hunky. Perhaps he could be *The Heart is a Lonely Hunter* – a book by Carson McCullers, which was made into a movie, but I haven't seen it. It's a very sad story about a deaf-mute who runs away and is befriended by various misfits and eventually commits suicide. No, forget it, I'm not going to name him that. How about *The Boyfriend*? Except, of course, he isn't.

'Are you looking forward to going back to Zimbabwe Presh?'

'Yes, of course, Gussie.' (He has a very attractive lisp and says yeth and of courth and Guthie.)

'But maybe we will stay here and the rest of the family will join us when they can.'

'Could you do that?'

'I don't know. I hope so as I've got a better chance of survival here.'

'What do you mean?'

'In my country, things are not so good. The hospitals are full of HIV Aids patients and there are not so many doctors or nurses. My mother is one of Zimbabwe's top surgeons. She thinks we should get out now, before things get even worse.'

'What sort of a doctor is your father?'

'A physician' (This sounds so cute with his lisp – 'phythithian' – I mustn't giggle.)

I wonder how it would be if that happened to me, if I had to leave my birth country to have the health care I need to survive. Mum would give up everything for me, I know, even her home. So would Daddy, I'm sure.

'I've been to Kenya. I loved it.'

'I have never been to Kenya, Gussie, but Zimbabwe is very beautiful. It has mountains and lakes. There are many wild animals and birds. Perhaps if I go home you can visit me?'

'Do you have elephants?'

'Many elephants.'

'I would love to come. And you must come to Cornwall. There are sandy beaches and rocky cliffs and little stone villages and harbours and we have dolphins and... and seals and seabirds. Do you like birds?'

'Yes, I have been birding with my school in the Eastern Highlands and Gonarezhou.'

He is as grave as a man. His eyes fill. I'm scared he might cry. Is he homesick for his country and missing his father and sisters? Will he ever go home? Will I ever go home? I hide my own sudden tears.

I read in a book called *The Snow Geese* that homesickness used to be recognised as a real illness. Soldiers serving a long way from home suffer from it and have to be kept busy so they don't have time to think. The same thing applies to boarding-school children. Keep them busy and they won't mope. It's not treated as an illness any more but it should be as it makes people sick with yearning, with melancholy and nostalgia (I've used it!) and a desperate need to see their home. I like moving to new places, it's exciting. I was never homesick when I was in Kenya or some other tropical country when I was little, but I think older people feel it badly sometimes, and need to be at home, or in their own country before they feel better. Even though Mum is old she's always been good about travelling with me and enjoys making a home out of a strange house.

Nomads can't have the gene that gives people homesickness. They move all the time, making camps along the journey. They must have the opposite of homesickness, homephobia.

I think of Cornwall as my real home now, not London where we lived with Daddy before Mummy left him. London means hospital to me now: tests, discomfort, waiting rooms, machines, sickness, pain, drugs, fear. The staff are all kind, they never make us feel that we are being a nuisance, but we are nevertheless worlds apart from them – the healthy, the fit and the free. I feel like I've lived here forever. We transplant patients are like asylum seekers or refugees, waiting for fate to decide what happens to us.

Precious is doing so well he's going home today. Or rather, he is being transferred to the hospital flat where his mother has been staying since his transplant.

'What's happening with your father, Presh?' He likes it when I call him that.

'What's happening with yours?' Oh very clever, Precious, I didn't realise he was aware of my parents' marital problems. My mother must have told his.

'He'll be back soon. We'll be staying at his flat. I'll keep in touch if you want.'

'Yes, I want.' We hug carefully and I smell pepper and medicated soap. I wonder what I smell of? I think English people are supposed to smell of butter. I think I smell of medicines and especially of the dreadful stuff I have to swallow to stop getting thrush. He is much taller and broader than Brett, older.

'See you, Gussie.' A blackbird pipes a warning as a dog barks from a car in the hospital car park. I wish I was getting out too. But I have plenty to plan. We'll have to register me at school so I can start in the summer term (I hope) and there's my uniform and stuff to buy. I wonder if they do cricket in the summer term? I quite like the idea of playing cricket. I could wear my England cricket cap that Alistair gave me. My maternal grandmother used to play cricket. Brett will be there – and Siobhan, of course. (Hope I'm not in her class.) But I mustn't live in the future, which might not happen. Live each moment now.

I have a hospital pet. It's a spider that lives in a high corner of my room. The cleaners haven't seen it and I'm not telling them. It's one of those very thin long-legged garden spiders. Its web is too far up for me to examine unfortunately, but I am aware of my spider busying herself, keeping house and hunting food, which must be hard in such an antiseptic environment. I haven't seen any flies. Her name is Eensy Weensy. Is she aware of me in my bed? It must look like a huge white ship marooned in a calm sea of blue floor. Will my ship ever get home? As long as I'm not shipwrecked I'll be fine. Voyages can be boring and exhausting, but they eventually end at a safe harbour. We went on a ship from Southampton to the Canaries once, when Daddy was still with us. It was awful, really rough, and Mum was seasick for three days, even when the ship stopped rolling. I was fine. Daddy and I played deck chess and watched for dolphins and whales but we didn't see any.

At least I have Rena Wooflie, my soft toy dog, to keep me company. She has been everywhere with me since I was three. Mummy bought her for me in Mombasa, when we were on our first winter away. She used to take me away from English winters because if I stay I get chest infections, which turn into bronchitis or pneumonia, so I miss school anyway. Being away each winter has probably been the only good thing about having a rare congenital heart disease. I have met people from Kenya, Thailand, the Canary Islands and the Seychelles.

I love Kenya best, because of the wild-life; I hope I will be able to go again one day soon. Once we saw a family of baboons crossing the road – the biggest holding the hand of a little one, just like humans, watching the traffic to see when it was safe. And I saw a huge monitor lizard in the bushes close to our house, and thought it was a dragon. I hid the cast off skin of a large cicada in Daddy's shoe as an April Fool trick, and it really fooled him. That was the only time he came out to be with us for a short time. He had to go back to work. Anyway, they didn't get on when he was with us. There were raised voices and clenched teeth – Mum's.

*

Precious hasn't been in to see me. Hope he's okay. Wish he was here – we could play chess. Mum hates chess. She's bored, I can tell. She's standing at the window and gazing out.

'What can you see, Mum?'

'Mmm?'

'Tell me what you see, I can't see anything from here.'

I'm feeling low and blue today and have come back to bed after the physio session.

'There's a gold carriage and four white horses with white plumes on their heads and they are stopping outside. I think they've come to take you to meet your prince.'

'What can you really see?'

'Not a lot. Sparrows pecking at something. Rain on the window pane.'

'Is the crow there?'

'Crow? No, no crow. Cars in the car park. It's like a Sunday afternoon when I was a child.'

'How do you mean?'

'Dull. Dull and grey and gloomy. No one having any fun. Fun is banned on Sundays, or it was then.'

'Tell me what you did when you were little.'

'I was a lucky child. In the holidays I played outside all day until teatime. I'd take jam sandwiches onto the beach for my lunch. When I was about ten I had a racing bike, second-hand, of course, I helped pay for it with my pocket money. I went everywhere on it, miles from home, into the countryside.'

'Weren't you ever attacked by paedophiles or perverts?'

'No, of course not.'

'So, why didn't you let me do that when I was ten?'

'Life isn't that simple any more, Gussie. Too many cars for a start.'

'Did you have animals?'

'We had lots of chickens, some rabbits, a cat and a dog.'

'Oh yes, Tiddles. I remember. What sort of dog was it?'

'Lion Pekinese – Foo. My Mother did a Terrible Thing. Foo was ill. Lost the use of his back legs, dragged himself around. She took him to the vet and left him there, she said, for the vet to make him better. But of course, the vet put him down... put him to sleep. I kept expecting him to come home and I worried about him. She should have told me. I can't remember how I found out.'

'Poor Mum.'

I suddenly start to worry about my cats. What if Charlie is ill and Claire takes her to the vet and has her put down? I'm not there to look after her. I bet she misses me. She always sleeps on my bed. Will Claire let her sleep on Gabriel's bed? Or Phaedra's or Troy's? Betya Rambo runs away: he's scared of everything.

'Tell me more about when you were little.'

'I'm Too Old, I can't remember.'

'Oh, go on, Mum. Tell me about the Veet.'

'The hair-remover? Oh, dear me, yes. It was my mother's. I was very young, about seven or eight. I thought it was face cream and I rubbed it all over my face and wiped it off after a little while. Then my mother caught sight of me. I had managed to remove both my eyebrows. She Was Furious.'

We laugh. We always laugh at that story. I love hearing the same stories over and over again, I don't know why. When I was little I loved Mum reading *The Three Billy Goats Gruff*. It was very scary but I loved it. There's a monster that lives under the bridge they have to cross to get to a green meadow. It's called a...? I must have slept a little. Mum has gone back to her hospital flat. I hope the crow has gone. I close my eyes and now I can't sleep. I keep thinking I might die if I fall asleep. This new heart will decide it doesn't want to beat inside my chest. My new lungs will let go my breath and forget to breathe in again. Will it hurt, dying? I will be… where, what? Not here anymore. Where will I be? Will my spirit or soul survive somewhere? Will I be simply a memory, a pain my mother and father have to bear for the rest of their lives? I think I might be having a panic attack. Or a heart attack. Maybe I'm rejecting again. My heart is racing and I can't stop moving my legs. There's a loud tapping at the windowpane, like the sharp beak of the crow. I press the button to call the nurse on night duty, Cynthia. She takes my temperature, blood pressure, pulse rate, etc; goes away and comes back with a pill and a drink of water with something in it and gives me an injection in my arm. I can hear her tights rubbing on her thighs. I wonder where nurses get those little watches they pin on their chests?

I'm a pincushion. I remember Grandma had one with a china lady on top – the velvet pincushion was her crinoline skirt. It's strange how some memories only last for that brief second you need to know them then disappear again into the dark recesses of the mind. At least my brain is okay – so far.

'You'll be fine, girlie, you'll be fine. Shall I call your Mummy?'

Cynthia is a large-bottomed, large-bosomed, woman with a skin like black satin and a voice like warm honey. I want her to hold me tight so I can feel safe. I imagine she would feel like a giant hot water bottle covered in satin.

'No, she'll be in bed now. I'll be okay, thank you.'

'I'll get you a hot milky drink, shall I, girlie?'

I cuddle Rena Wooflie and nod.

'Cynthia, is there anything at the window?'

'What'ya mean, girlie? Not'in' is at the window.' She draws back the curtain to look. 'Only the wind and the rain – your awful winter.'

It's called a troll – the monster under the bridge. My brain seems to process information or memories during the night when I sleep and comes up with answers in the morning. Very clever.

Precious is here. My mum and his have gone for a coffee. Precious shows me a letter he has had from his sister, Grace, who is eleven. His other sister, Blessed, is eight.

Dear Precious,
I am well and so is Blessed, but we miss you very much.
Daddy takes us to school and our maid collects us at
the end of the day. We have electricity for two hours
a day most days and it is difficult to do homework
by candlelight, so teacher has stopped giving it to us!
My friend's father died last week and we went to his
funeral. It was very sad. Now my friend cannot come
to school any more because her mother cannot pay her
fees. On the roadside people are selling coffins. I hope
you come home soon.
With all my love and prayers,
Your loving sister, Grace

Eeensy Weensy is still weaving her webs and living on my ceiling. I understand now how some English king or other took comfort in the company of a spider, and learned to be patient as she was, waiting for that one insect to land on her carefully woven web. Was it the same king that burnt the cakes? My knowledge of history is rubbish.

I wonder what age they are doing at school? I better ask Brett.

There's a schoolroom here, with paper and crayons and paints, a small library and a computer – yay – hopefully someone will show me how to use it soon. Precious wants to learn too.

Katy says it's not unusual for PT patients to feel nauseated. It's the drugs. It's boring, though, because feeling sick stops me from reading, or doing anything else. My head is spinning and my stomach feels as if it will empty itself any moment. Being hospitalised is mostly boring – there is so much hanging around, waiting for treatment – punctuated with fear and pain. Like being a soldier or sailor at war, I suppose. There they are hanging around in a bunker or whatever, cleaning their boots and painting coal white, or scrubbing decks if they are at sea, and then suddenly they are having bombs lobbed at them or they are shooting and being shot at.

I feel a bit better today. Not so jumpy and twitchy, or nauseated, but I can still see the raven or whatever it is. Perhaps I should feed it and then it wouldn't be so menacing. It might as well be carrying a scythe. I've never been any good at telling big, black birds apart. Maybe it's a carrion crow. It's not a jackdaw. Jackdaws are quite small and cocky and talk a lot. I like jackdaws. I remember one in Fore Street at the end of the summer. It stood on a lamp attached to a cottage and was chattering away to itself very loudly, with lots of different sounds. A monologue. It was so unusual that visitors were actually stopping to look up and watch it. I wish I could understand bird languages. Is it easy for robins to understand what starlings or rooks are saying or do they only understand other robins? And do robins in foreign countries understand what our robins say? Someone on the radio said that human beings are the only creatures with language but I don't agree. It's odd that we can translate foreign human languages but not animals' methods of communication. Herring gulls have the most interesting and varied calls I have heard in a bird. They seem to laugh, cry, scream with anger, chuckle, chat, talk to themselves, grumble, grieve, threaten, canoodle. I do miss them. In London there are black-headed gulls and terns, who screech and shriek rather bad-temperedly, but they don't chat to each other like herring gulls do.

I go to have x-rays and cardiographs and other tests and meet three children who are waiting for transplants with their parents. They all have the same look – the parents – anxious, tense. I think the parents worry more than the patients.

I am up and about and feeling great. A walk around the hospital garden with Mum and... no crow. Well, there are yellow-beaked rooks in a big tree near the road building nests like witch's brooms, but the night-crow is not on the tree outside my window. I spot lots of sparrows and starlings, one robin and a wren. Oh, and I heard a broody chicken. Must be from a garden somewhere nearby. Grandma had chickens and I recognise a broody chicken when I hear one. *Corr, cocococor. Cocococorrr.* Or maybe it has just laid an egg and is proud of it.

The sun is shining, big white clouds rush across a blue sky and all's well with my world. Not Precious's world, though. His blood sugar is out of control, his kidneys are packing up and he is back in hospital for them to sort out his treatment. He's having dialysis. It's not an unusual problem for post heart transplant patients. I'm lucky I haven't had any kidney problems – yet.

I am allowed to go outside the hospital grounds with Mum, who pushes me in the wheelchair as it's quite a trek. I feel like a fraud, but Mum and Katy insist I am transported this way. We go to the river. There's a grey heron, tall and still, on the other bank. Reeds swaying. Coots and moorhens bustle along, black feathers fluffed out by the wind, and mallards fly low past us. The world is so beautiful! I want to do what Mary Oliver says – 'kneel down and give thanks'… or was it Raymond Carver? Some American writer. I get out of the wheelchair and walk a little way along the bank.

I feel full of life, oozing with life, bursting with life, exploding with life, fainting with life. '*My cup of life brimmeth over.*' Bliss – like that story by Katherine Mansfield. Such perfect happiness simply in being alive. I can't imagine ever being happier than I am now. Except I suppose I shouldn't be feeling this way as my friend Precious is very ill.

I mooch, doing nothing for the rest of the day, reading and dozing and watching the telly. I felt that I was totally recovered this morning, but now I'm exhausted. Beat Mum at Scrabble, though. She now owes me £216.

CHAPTER FOUR

VESTIGE—A FOOTPRINT; A TRACE; A SURVIVING TRACE OF WHAT HAS
ALMOST DISAPPEARED; A REDUCED AND FUNCTIONLESS STRUCTURE,
ORGAN, ETC, REPRESENTING WHAT WAS ONCE USEFUL AND DEVELOPED

EUPHORIA—AN EXAGGERATED FEELING OF WELL-BEING, ESP. IRRATIONAL
OR GROUNDLESS

I NOW KNOW the difference between big black birds – at least
in theory. Ravens are the largest – about 61 cm – bigger than
buzzards, and they are rare. They have a wedge-shaped tail
in flight. In *The Natural History of Selborne* there's a sad
story about a big old tree that always had a raven's nest in
the top branches and the local boys couldn't get to it because
of a huge lump in the trunk that they couldn't climb around,
so the nest was safe. But the tree was cut down and the
mother bird sat on her eggs even when the tree was felled,
and she died.

Carrion crow – 44–51 cm. The face is feathered. Crows
are solitary, not sociable like rooks, who build their nests
in a village of trees, not too close and not too far from each
other. Young rooks have to behave or they are driven out by
their elders.

Rooks, like people, build towns for self-protection. Their
worst enemy is the carrion crow. One pair can destroy an
entire rookery, driving the parents from their nests and
eating the eggs and young.

Rooks are about 46 cm long, wholly black, except for a
greyish face, bare of feathers. Usually gregarious. Nests like
large witch's brooms.

Carrion crow is similar in size, has a thicker beak and

is wholly black. Hooded crow is the size of rook but with light-grey body and black wings and tail, black head and straggly black bib.

Jackdaw is smaller than rook, but hangs about with them. Seen in pairs, amorous. Dark grey. Lighter grey neck side and nape. Eye is greyish white. On ground struts around with upright posture. They are conversational, with many cries – short and cutting and quite pleasing. Some harsh and hoarse – *Kya, kyack kyaar*, and harsher *tschreh*. Chatter quietly together and bill and coo.

Jackdaw is smallest of the crows – 30–34 cm. Dark grey, not black. Lighter neck-side and nape, short dark beak, pairs for life, amorous. (That's true, I often see them in pairs canoodling – one of Grandpop's words – side by side on street lamps.) Likes chimneys. Dense flocks – like pigeons. Alarm call is furious, hoarse, drawn out. *Chaiihr.* Cackling together in large flocks at night. His wings give quicker, sharper strokes, *Chack chack* – his call. Jackdaw has pearly-white eyes. He steals baby birds as well as eating insects and grubs. Small, rounder head and dark, shorter beak; grey under wing; likes chimneys.

I'll never remember all of that.

I need to see them all walking around together with labels on, flying together with labels on and sitting in trees with labels on.

I only notice my scary crow when I am lying in bed feeling sick and sad.

I can now walk to the end of the corridor on my own. Hurray!

I've been watching a movie on the television in my room. I usually don't, as it is high on the wall and it makes my neck ache. Also I prefer quiet so I can read or play Scrabble with

Mum. But *Hook* was on, with Dustin Hoffman as Captain Hook, so we watched it together.

It was cool.

I wonder why so many actors are short? I've made a list (no children, dwarfs or female actors allowed).

Dustin Hoffman
Danny de Vito
Tom Cruise
Alan Ladd (had to stand on a box to kiss some actress)
Woody Allen
Humphrey Bogart
Michael J Fox
Mickey Rooney
Al Pacino
Richard Dreyfus
Gene Kelly
Fred Astaire
Paul Newman

And I happen to know that Pablo Picasso and Joseph Stalin were only 5 ft 4 in. I think Napoleon was short too.

Daddy is quite short; maybe that's why he's good at acting. Or are all short men show offs? I'm a dreadful show-off, Grandma used to say. If they were taking me to meet one of their friends she would say, 'Don't forget your hanky and don't show off.' I was very young then. I am shorter than other girls my age and I have probably inherited my show-offedness from Daddy.

Precious is improving. He is off the kidney machine and back to his healthy colour. The yellowy brown tinge he had when his kidneys failed was like the colour of the sky in St

Ives when there's a storm brewing. He still feels weak, he says. We play chess and he beats me. I'm crap at chess. I say we must play more Scrabble as it will help his English. It helped me when I was little and learning new words. Mum made me look up words I thought might exist so my vocabulary is not bad for a twelve year old. (Brett's mum told me that. She should know, she's an English teacher. Well, she's Australian, but she teaches English.)

Today I leave hospital. I can't believe it. Some of the transplant team are here to wave goodbye – the ones who aren't too busy. I cry a few tears. It's been like an unusually long holiday at a hotel with lots of staff, a good gym, but no sunshine. Alistair has taken more leave and comes all the way from Cornwall to collect me and Mum but he refuses to put the flashing light on top of his car like he did when he drove me here. Mum says he's a spoilsport. We are going to stay at Daddy's flat and Alistair will be with us for three days. He looks less like a horse these days, more bovine and sweet looking. He's being gentle with me, and with Mum, who keeps bursting into tears. Anyone would think I had died instead of surviving.

It is scary that I won't be surrounded by nurses and doctors who know what to do if anything goes wrong, but I'll still have to go back twice a week for check-ups and physiotherapy and once a week I'll have heart and lung biopsies, ECGs and other tests. I think that's right, it's complicated, but Mum has all the details. I was lucky to have my transplant the first time I was called. Katy says some people have as many as five 'shouts' or 'dry runs', even getting as far as having a general anaesthetic before the operation is cancelled. That would be pretty bad, waking up without anything having been done and having to go home and wait to go through the whole thing again. That sort of thing happened to me once, with my operation to build a pulmonary artery. When I was opened up, the surgeon could see I had no vestige of an artery to build on, so they had to close me up again without doing anything. That was when I went on the transplant list.

I don't remember much about the preparations on the night I came in for the transplant. I had lots of blood taken, along with loads of other tests, and I had to bathe in disinfectant. The oxygen I was given made me feel light-headed and giggly. Mum wasn't allowed to kiss me but I remember blowing her kisses as I was wheeled into the theatre. I don't think she saw, she was crying onto Alistair's shoulder. The last thing I remember is that I felt cold and wished they'd let me keep my socks on.

I feel I've been imprisoned for years and now I'm free, out on bail anyway. All the people with no worries, laughing and chatting, kids running and playing – they don't know how lucky they are.

London is grey after Cornwall. I miss the big sky and the blue bay. But there are yellow and purple crocuses under the bare trees, a promise of spring. So many people walking briskly in the wintry wind, healthy people with hearts and lungs working properly. *I'll* be able to do that soon.

Dad's flat is large and expensive looking, the garden floor and ground floor of a Victorian house in Southend Green, a couple of minutes to Hampstead Heath. Great for my new exercise regime: walks building up to twenty minutes or more a day. Mum and I will know the Heath well by the time we leave. I have Daddy's bedroom and Mum sleeps on one of the two enormous sofas in the sitting room – actually, it's a sofa-bed. I feel rather guilty about having the double bed while Alistair is here, but he is being nice about it. I'm glad he's here for Mum. At the same time I'm sad that Daddy isn't here, and we aren't one happy family. I light a candle for the donor of my new organs. 'Whoever you are – thank you.' We celebrate my new life with a carrot cake from the patisserie in the village. *It's a Wonderful Life* but I'm tearful, I don't know why; the counsellor at the hospital says it's normal, and I mustn't worry. One of the drugs I'm taking makes my mood swing wildly, one moment I'm euphoric and the next in despair. I must remember that it isn't permanent depression; it will pass when I eventually come off this particular drug.

Alistair has done loads of shopping. He got me lovely fresh fruit, strawberries and raspberries, plums and peaches – all out of season. We are having an Indian takeaway, but I've gone off curry. I seem to have lost my sense of taste. I wonder if my donor didn't like spicy food? Mum says I shouldn't have anything too hot anyway, just gentle food. So in the end I have only plain rice with pappadoms and dhall and a lovely tomato salad, made by Alistair, and chopped banana. We have to eat at the dining table, not sitting on a sofa watching TV, as the furniture is upholstered in cream suede and we're sure to spill something on it. Mum suggests throwing blankets over it all so we won't have to worry. But Daddy only has duvets.

We watch a movie on Daddy's home cinema screen, which takes up one wall of the sitting room. He works in the movie industry. Well, actually, he works at a film archive, but he is still trying to make movies. He did make one once, but it wasn't released. We watch *The Wizard of Oz*. I have seen it about six times. The first time, I was five and I screamed the place down and had to be carried out. It was the wicked witch, of course, with her horrid, green face.

Mum and Alistair are sitting at one end of the enormous

sofa, cuddling and drinking sparkling wine – Mum is scared of even *opening* a bottle of *red* wine in case it spills – and I'm at the other end, tucked up with a duvet and Rena Wooflie. She is looking smart, as Mum washed her when I was in ICU. I had no idea her checked dress was such a bright pink.

I miss my cats. I wonder – if I phoned Mrs Thomas, would she get Charlie to meow to me? Cats have no understanding of time and distance. Will they forgive me for leaving them? They might have forgotten who I am when they see me. They might prefer to be with the Darlings in their huge garden, with chickens and rabbits and ducks to chase. They won't want to go back to Bowling Green and the tiny garden there.

My first bath outside hospital: Mum helps me in and out. My scar is quite sensational. Still a little bit weepy, the incision – and me. We have to keep a close watch to make sure there's no infection. My left arm hurts when I lift it; and my right leg, for some reason. I had been told that having the clips out would be painful but it wasn't too bad. Fear of pain is often worse than the pain itself, in my experience.

First night in a civilian bed. It's so soft and comfortable. No machines humming and lights flickering. It feels strange.

I was in danger of becoming institutionalised.

Mum's travel clock says 4 a.m. I get up for a wee and sit on the lavatory, simply enjoying the fact that I'm alive. A small, beige moth drowns in the puddle of damp by the bath plug. Another flings itself again and again at the ceiling light.

I look at my hands. The skin is torn where I bite my nails. The central heating is off but the towel rail is heated and I don't feel cold. London at night is quieter than Cornwall, but then there's the far off siren of an ambulance. I wonder who is sick, and will they die? In Cornwall there's the wind fighting to get in the windows and doors, the waves crashing on the beach, gulls calling to each other in the dark. If I was there, Charlie would be on my lap. She doesn't allow me to go to the bathroom without her.

A line from one of Mum's bathroom books – 'Poetry is truth seen with passion.'

And from my bathroom reading: 'Moth caterpillars and larvae have very particular food needs. Some live only on nettles, some on elm leaves, or oak, some on chestnut.'

Perhaps I'll be a lepidopterist. It sounds such fun – You are a night creature like fox, badger, bat. You have a large white sheet spread out on the leafy floor of a wood or wherever and a powerful mercury vapour lamp. Moths are for some unknown reason attracted to the light. They arrive on the sheet like dancers and clowns tumbling into a brightly lit circus ring, fluttering their papery wings, quivering and shivering their furry bodies. 'Moths... live in a world of smells. They also have tympanal organs, sensitive to sound, which are situated on their abdomens or thorax. The moth "hears" vibrations.' (That's from *Wildwood* by Roger Deakin.)

More cards today, from Ginnie and from Brett's parents, who've sent me a video of bird behaviour and song. Mum won't let me watch it until Dad shows us how to work his equipment as it's all so professional looking. But I can easily do it. Adults are useless at modern technology.

Daddy phones from some foreign place with sounds of partying going on behind him.

'How's The Great Gussie?' He's referring to *The Great Gatsby,* of course, one of his favourite movies. He has a huge collection of old movies.

'I'm good, Daddy. I like your flat, it's ace. Lurv the cinema screen.'

'Yeah, yeah, good, good. Make yourselves at home, that's right. Give me to Lara, honeybun.'

Mum takes the phone with a sigh, goes into the other room and listens.

He always wanted me to call him Jackson and Mum Lara, but I prefer to use Mum and Daddy. It makes me feel safer, somehow. I don't want him to be a friend – I need him to be my father. He's never been good at that, though. Alistair is much more father material. He's a family doctor and Mum is keen on him. He's kind. I think he's a bit embarrassed at sleeping with my mother in the next room, but I'm broad-minded. At least he is nearer to Mum's age than Daddy's girlfriends are to his. Daddy seems to only want trophies half his age.

CHAPTER FIVE

THERE'S A SAD and sombre atmosphere in the cardiac rehabilitation clinic today. Two people have died this week waiting for donors – one was Pete, a window cleaner I met about three times when we were both in wheelchairs, waiting around. He was always attached to oxygen tanks but still looked really grey. He has – had, three small children. He was forty-one. The other person was an eighteen-month-old baby girl. The team are all subdued and sad, but were really pleased to see me. It's awful how guilty I feel at being alive, like the only survivor of an earthquake or a plane crash. I do stretching, stationary bike and arm ergometer exercises. It feels so good being able to breathe.

I hear one of the patients asking a physio, 'Have you got a dog?' and she says, 'No, but I've got a horrible son.'

I didn't see Precious today. I missed him. Hope he's okay.

I have to be careful not to get viruses or infections, as I am immune-suppressed and will get ill. So I have to stay away from people with coughs and colds. I hope that doesn't mean that I'm not going to be able to go to school.

On the way back to the flat, Alistair has to stop the car so that I can open the door and vomit. I've never been carsick in my life. Mum and Alistair discuss whether to take me straight back to hospital.

My incision is sore and my chest hurts from the retching.

'I'm fine, don't take me back there, please.'

'I think she'll be okay,' says Alistair.

With the windows open, I do feel better. Mum finds a tissue, dips it in bottled water and cools my forehead and pulse points.

'Don't fuss, Mum.'

I take the tissue from her. I'm clammy, but I don't think I'll be sick again.

I think it's the drugs. They all have side effects but they're necessary to stop my body from rejecting my new organs. I'll have to take them for the rest of my life, but that's all right – I wouldn't have a REST OF MY LIFE without my new heart and lungs and all these drugs.

'If she's no better when we get there, we'll phone the hospital and see what they say.'

'Okay.' Mum looks relieved.

I'm glad Alistair is with us. He phones anyway, even though I feel fine, and they say to wait and see how I feel in an hour or two, but I feel absolutely okay so there's no panic.

When Alistair goes back to Cornwall, we use Daddy's car to get to and from the hospital. It's swish – a black convertible sports car. Shame it's too chilly to have the roof off.

Precious is at the clinic today. He's looking well and smiles broadly when he sees me. 'Guthie, Guthie,' he calls from the other end of the corridor. It's good to see him. We work side by side at physio. Dolores is my favourite physiotherapist. She is a slender beautiful Ghanaian who never stops talking and laughing. She makes me work hard and I hate it at the time but feel grateful afterwards.

I watch Precious do his exercises, his arms the colour of conkers just out of the shell. The sight of the pale soles of his large flat feet somehow make me feel happier. Precious has heard from his father. He's trying to get a job in England.

They have a big house in the best part of Harare, but if it is sold they won't be able to take that money out of the country. So they must think hard before making a decision.

Afterwards, in the café, Agnes tells Mum more about their predicament. There are food riots in Harare, as well as other towns in Zimbabwe. People can't afford to buy their staple foods – mealie maize, cooking oil. Government troops are using tear gas to disperse protestors. Doctors and nurses aren't getting paid. Drugs aren't available for the sick.

'It's a nightmare. I think many people will starve,' she says. 'My husband is in danger because he vociferously opposes Mugabe and Zanu-PF. Members of the MDC and Mugabe's political opponents are arrested and tortured. He must leave...' she is sobbing, 'he must bring our girls here. If he cannot work here we will go to Australia or New Zealand. They must leave...'

Mum gets her a cup of tea.

'You need whisky, not tea,' she says, and Precious's mum smiles through her tears.

'What's the MDC?' I ask.

'The Movement for Democratic Change,' says Agnes and blows her nose.

I am surrounded by sadness these days, when I should be enveloped in happiness. After all, I have survived. I am a survivor. I only have one real problem – keeping well. Most people in the world have life-threatening problems – war, starvation, fear of imprisonment or torture, no clean water, fatal diseases with no hope of treatment, like Aids and typhoid fever; earthquake, floods, drought. They might be homeless, exiled, old and poor, or motherless, orphans with no hope. Life is very hard for most of the earth's population. We are very lucky here. My Grandpop always said that. We have freedom of speech; we don't get put in prison when we disagree with the government of the day. Our poets aren't tortured as they are in some parts of the world. Dictators are frightened of poets because poets say what they think. Their poems can make people into dissidents. I think poets are great. I really must write some more poems.

I think of being in Kenya when I was little: the warmth of the air, the smells of pepper, the monkeys and butterflies.

'You'll be able to work in the UK, won't you?' Mum asks Agnes.

'Maybe later, but I must get help to look after my daughters. And I cannot leave my son to care for himself just yet.'

Here is a poem I have written about Kenya.

Bamburi

I am on the beach all day,
find coral, cowries, puffer fish washed in by the sea,
watch monkeys fly from the sausage tree.
Catch huge millipedes to place on my arms,
race big butterflies folding fan-like through the palms,
chase dragons stalking dappled gloom of casuarina,
walk with the tall baboons.
Cotton-wool air filters scent of pepper,
sweet potato, banana, mango, papaya,
coconut, Mombasa meat market.

'What's vociferous, Mum?'
'What do you think it means?'
'Voice... loud-voiced?'
'More or less, yes. Look it up in the dictionary.'

VOCIFEROUS — MAKING A LOUD OUTCRY; NOISY OR CLAMOROUS

We're having our morning walk on Parliament Hill, wrapped up against a gusting east wind. The trees are still bare, their thin branches like arms stretched up to the sky begging for sun and warmth. Dry brown leaves rustle and rush across the grass like demented hamsters. A large party of pigeons rise from the grass in front of us. They flap around our heads in a blur of blue and grey, smelling of musty chicken food. (Grandma used to cook potato skins and porridge oats in a pressure cooker for her chickens. I quite like the smell.) There's a woman with a little boy flying a kite. She looks sad. I wonder if her husband has left them. Mum used to fly kites with me here when we lived in London, when I was much younger. Where was Daddy then?

We watch the yellow kite tug at the string, the woman doing all the work, the little boy wandering off to chase a small gathering of Black-headed gulls, which run and rise together squealing. We stop to rest for a moment on a wooden bench. *Wayne loves Amy. Scott is fit.* Is it graffiti when it's incised on wood? A flurry of leaves blows in a circle, a mini whirlwind. The road where Daddy lives looks like it's been laid with a leaf-patterned laminate.

'Mum, I'm going to phone and see if Summer's around. She might come and see me.' Summer is the only one of my old school friends in London that I have kept in touch with, sort of. Though she doesn't know about my transplant.

No reply. I expect she's away for the weekend. I don't really have any other friends now in London. I can't wait to go back to Cornwall and walk along a beach or go birding with Brett.

Today, I find a peacock butterfly in my bedroom. Poor thing, it's much too cold for it outside, but now it's awake I have to let it out into the garden. Who knows what will become of it – it could be part of a robin's lunch. It won't survive long, but at least it will have a moment's freedom in the cold blue sky.

Daddy is back from Hungary but is staying elsewhere – with his latest girlfriend, Annika (leggy, blonde, big tits, not her own). He's so predictable. There are photos of her pouting in his room. She should be wearing a T-shirt like the ones I've seen in a shop in St Ives, with a message on – *I wish these were brains* – an arrow pointing to her tits. He's taken his car, though, and we're renting one.

Mum invited three of her old London friends to supper, but one has cancelled as she has a cold and I mustn't be exposed to germs. There's so many things to be scared of post-transplant, or rather, be aware of. We're having chicken, lentil and vegetable soup, a green salad and a lemon meringue pie. I made the salad with roasted sunflower seeds on top, lemon and olive oil. I mustn't have mayonnaise as it's high-risk for food poisoning, ditto raw egg, pâté and partially cooked meats. I don't really like pink meat anyway.

Mimi is half-Italian, half-Australian and larger than life – which means she talks loudly, swears a lot and wears outrageous clothes, false eyelashes and scarlet nails. She's *The Italian Job*. Celeste, fierce and stern and chic is from Paris. She wears a black trouser suit and has short blonde hair and pale make-up – *The French Connection*. She smokes, but Mum doesn't let her do it indoors, sends her outside in the rain and shuts the door so the smoke doesn't drift in. Mum is... I haven't decided what movie Mum is yet. *Mommie Dearest*! Of course. I must ask Mum if her name really is Lara or if it's Laura or Lorna. Daddy might have made her change it to Lara because of *Doctor Zhivago*. I could call Alistair Dr Z maybe? What is Daddy, though? *The Vanishing*.

I go to bed early with my book and Rena Wooflie – *The Big Sleep* – no, an ordinary sleep, I hope. The Big Sleep means death.

It's good to hear Mum laughing. Mimi's voice becomes more Australian and less Italian when she's had a few glasses of wine.

'Kill for a ciggie,' I hear her say. 'Gave it up New Year and I've put on ten kilos.'

Valentine's Day – I forgot. One card, hand-made, with a red heart and blue arrow surrounded by kisses – luv yu lots, xxx no signature – must be Gabriel. And a box of flowers from the Scillies – Paper Whites – from Brett. The small card inside says: '*Remember the islands? We'll go again one day, Brett x.*'

The flowers smell of cold sea air and dark earth. I phone to thank him and he tells me they have frog and toad spawn in their pond. I love tadpoles: that big black mouth with a tail. I wonder if our tiny pond has any life in it? We should have, as a giant toad lives in the grow-bag under our garden seat. I can hear seagulls at his end of the phone. I do miss the sound of gulls. Why hasn't Daddy got an animal? His flat seems so un-homelike without even a single goldfish.

Mum has a card too, from Alistair. She's rather old to have a Valentine's card. It makes her smile and cry. She won't let me see what it says.

Back at the cardiac rehab clinic (I have to go back to hospital twice a week for six weeks). I'm doing fine, they say. But when I mention bird-watching and then the pigeons on Parliament Hill, one of the doctors tells me to stay away from them.

'But why?

'*C. Neoformans.*'

'What's that?'

'*Cryptococcus Neoformans* – it's a fungus that's a major threat to people with weak immune systems. It appears in bird droppings, and you might breathe it in. Caged birds are to be avoided too. You don't have a parrot, do you?'

I shake my head. Grandpop had a parrot and I was scared of its sharp beak. It was jealous of me.

'Budgie? Canary?'

'No.'

'Better not take chances, Gussie.'

I think of the thick cloud of dusty birds and hope I haven't inhaled the deadly fungus. Oh dear, does that mean I can never get close to flocks of any birds or is it only pigeons I must beware of? 'Be afraid. Be very afraid.' (Geena Davis, in *The Fly.*)

One of Daddy's favourite directors is Alfred Hitchcock, who made a film about birds suddenly ganging up against people and attacking them. It was originally a story by Daphne Du Maurier, who lived in Cornwall and wrote *Rebecca* and lots of other romantic adventure stories.

I've had a terrible thought: what about Paradise Park? It's one of my favourite places in Cornwall. They have all sorts of birds there in huge aviaries and they breed threatened species like choughs. One of the staff gave me some blue and green macaw feathers once. Should I throw them away? I don't want to.

On our walk today we went into the corner shop and a small boy in front of us in the queue was grizzling because he wanted to eat his bar of chocolate straight away.

'When we've gone past the witch's house you can have it,' his mother said.

When I was little we used to drive past a house with a neon 'Guest House' sign, and I used to hide my eyes in terror because I thought it said ghost house. Presumably *he* isn't frightened of witches. We walk as far as the pond and watch the swans, feathers ruffled forwards as they drift in the strong wind. They always look cross, like Flo, our alpha female cat. She has black spots each side of her nose and they make her look like a bad-tempered swan.

Joggers run past with red legs.

Precious and his Mum are very excited. His father is coming to London soon with the two girls. His mum looks ecstatic at the prospect of seeing them; they have been apart for nine months.

There are daffodils everywhere on the way home – in window boxes and on little front lawns and in swathes on the Heath. I like the ordinary single flowers, not double ones that fall over when they are wet. No, I like all of them – living lovely flowers, the brightness of them. After each dark winter we are given daffodils, like a huge smile from God. Except that I don't think I believe in God. I don't know what I believe in. I suppose I believe in the human spirit. Our ability to overcome bad experiences, like the loss of loved ones. I am feeling less unhappy about the death of my grandparents, for example. We have to say goodbye to our old people when they come to the end of their lives. They have to make room for the rest of us. It's sad, but it's life. And I am alive. Mum says the daffs are blooming early this year especially for me.

'Mum, do you think Precious's family had to pay for his transplant?'

'I don't know, darling, I imagine they did.'

I wonder how much a new heart costs? And how much for

a pair of lungs. And they would have to pay for the surgeon's time, the anaesthetist's time. And then there's paying for the nursing and drugs he'll have to take for the rest of his life.

'We didn't have to pay anything for my new heart and lungs, did we?'

'No Guss, our taxes help pay for the National Health Service so all our treatment is free – sort of.'

CHAPTER SIX

METAPHOR—A FIGURE OF SPEECH BY WHICH A THING IS SPOKEN OF AS BEING THAT WHICH IT ONLY RESEMBLES, AS WHEN A FEROCIOUS MAN IS CALLED A TIGER

PSYCHOANALYST—ONE WHO PRACTICES PSYCHOANALYSIS, A METHOD OF INVESTIGATION AND PSYCHOTHERAPY WHEREBY NERVOUS DISEASES OR MENTAL AILMENTS ARE TRACED TO FORGOTTEN HIDDEN CONCEPTS IN THE PATIENT'S MIND AND TREATED BY BRINGING THESE TO LIGHT

The Geometer (earth measurer) moths or Geometridae are a family of the order Lepidoptera. Its caterpillar lacks most of the prolegs of other Lepidoptera caterpillars. Equipped with appendages at both ends of the body, a caterpillar will clasp with its front legs and draw up the hind end, then clasp with the hind end (prolegs) and reach out again for a new front attachment, so it looks like it is measuring its journey. The caterpillars are accordingly called loopers, spanworms, or inchworms (they are about one inch long). They tend to be grey, green or brownish and hide from predators by fading into the background or resembling twigs. Some have humps or filaments. They are seldom hairy or gregarious. Typically they eat leaves. However, some eat lichen, flowers or pollen. Some, such as the Eupithecia, are even carnivorous.

from a pocket-book on moths

I do like moths. I had no idea the inchworm was a moth caterpillar.

There was a song about inchworms measuring marigolds in that old Danny Kaye musical, *Hans Christian Andersen* – he wonders why they don't stop to look at how beautiful the marigolds are. I always think marigolds smell of raw rhubarb – earthy and sharp. I suppose the lyrics mean that you shouldn't try only to scientifically assess something that's lovely; you should enjoy it for itself. You can't measure beauty.

Moths have such lovely names: latticed heath; brimstone moth; purple thorn; scalloped hazel; swallow-tailed moth; feathered thorn; peppered moth; dotted border; mottled umber; clouded border; willow beauty; clouded silver; the dingy footman, the flame shoulder; the dew moth; bordered white; common white wave; light emerald; (I don't like spring cankerworm much, though); small fan-footed wave; cream wave; small dusty wave; juniper carpet; may highflyer; winter moth; the streak; ash pug; lime-speck pug. There's loads more. Naming them must be a bit like naming decorating paints. You have to keep coming up with interesting but descriptive words, like Apple-Blossom White, or Coated Tongue Pink. I made up that last one. I could make up my own colour chart easily: Squirrel Red and, of course, Squirrel Grey; Pulmonary Atresia Grey (mauve grey like I used to be); Post-op Pink; Nurse White; London Grass (that's a sort of grey-brown rather than green); Hospital Green – or Theatre Gown Green; Jealousy – a violent lime green (Bridget feels in colour); Painful Purple (see above); Silver Lining; Lightning; (the last two are shades of white); Rain Grey. I'll think up more, later. It's the sort of thing I do when I can't sleep and I've read too much and made my eyes sore.

That's something that hasn't improved – my eyesight. Obviously my donor didn't have 100 per cent vision.

My dreams are disturbing. Being lost, not being able to

get home, losing my mother and father and cats. Being in a foreign land and not speaking the language. I wish Mum would get a boyfriend who was a psychoanalyst, so I could ask him about my dreams. Alistair is an ordinary doctor, a GP, good with aches and pains, disease and injuries, but he hasn't been trained to deal with bad dreams. I'm always relieved when I wake up and find I am safe in bed with Mum close by.

I've written a poem about one of my bad dreams.

Blackbirds Dying

A leafless tree
noisy with blackbirds
in a winter dawn.

Silence sinks like a knife.
One by one they fall.
Dead birds blacken the lawn.

'Mum, when are you going to have your operation?'

'What operation?'

'The operation to remove your fibroids.'

'How do you know about my fibroids?'

'Mrs Thomas. I heard you telling her.' (Mum has heavy periods and needs to have fibroids removed from her uterus.)

'Plenty of time to think about that. I'll have it when you're better. No rush.'

'You sure?'

'Sure I'm sure.' She goes to the bathroom. She spends ages in the bathroom, but luckily there are two in Dad's flat.

I know my donor heart and lungs came from a woman under twenty, but I don't know any more than that. If

I decide I want to know more I can write a letter to the family, via the transplant coordinator, and they can decide whether to answer the letter. I feel that I am grieving for the person who died, and I have a right to know who it was. But if it happened to be a murderer, would I want to know? Or a drug addict? Or someone who was so unhappy they committed suicide? Maybe I shouldn't know. A donor has to be brain-dead, their next of kin have to agree to allow their organs to be used. Difficult for them, to be thinking of saving someone else's life. There aren't enough donated organs for all the sick people waiting for a transplant. That's why so many die while they're still waiting. Even if I don't survive longer than a year or two, I'm grateful that I have been given this gift of time. I can't wait to breathe in the clean sea air of home.

Another blip. A chest infection. I feel faint, breathless. Ill. Back to hospital. I'm scared. Mum's scared. The transplant nurses are brilliant. Katy and Soo Yung are sorting out my medication and tell us it happens all the time and not to worry. I am given strong antibiotics. Mum is staying in a flat in the grounds again. I feel like I live here now, not Cornwall.

Haven't seen Precious. Or anyone, except Mum and hospital staff. Will I ever be well enough to go home? I'm in a different room this time, a pale yellow one, but the huge crow is still on a tree outside my window. He doesn't caw like ordinary crows. He sits sullen and menacing in his punk feathers, staring in my window. I turn to face the wall. Perhaps he'll go away if I don't look. I'll make a photograph of him when I'm feeling more human.

At least I felt human at Daddy's flat, not like some sort of robot. Mum sits with me for most of the day and I'm still pretty sorry for myself, but Katy said I must remain positive, and it's unlike me to mope. I can't help it. I feel like a snail without a shell, or a bird with a broken wing. I could die here in this grey place, with no beach outside the window, no herring gulls calling. Only sirens and sick people, flashing blue lights and noisy helicopters.

I want so much to be back home, Charlie, Flo and Rambo competing for my attention. Are they being loved enough by the Darlings? Is Gabriel grooming them? Charlie loves to be combed, especially under her chin on her white throat, where fleas gather to suck her blood.

Alistair has checked on our house and says the apple tree is nearly in blossom. Spring comes earlier to Cornwall than London. I wonder if the starling still sits on the telegraph wire and whistles and clicks to the Sky God? Are there gulls on the roof?

Only three weeks to go before we were supposed to go back to Cornwall. Will I still be able to, or will this setback delay things? Oh dear, I'm crying again and it hurts my head and throat.

I'm out of hospital, joyful as a caged bird set free. Mummy is pretty pleased too. Alistair has come up again just to take us back to Daddy's flat, though he can't stay for more than one night. I am to take it easy for a few days. Suits me, I've got plenty of books to keep me going, and I'm beating Mum at Scrabble almost every time we play. We play for money: £1 for every point. She owes me £346 already. I better let her win some back or she'll refuse to play.

Each day I feel stronger. I walk a little further onto the Heath, Mum holding my arm. Ducks squabble on the pond; swans look down their noses at them; rooks do aero-acrobatics. The Heath is still wintry-looking with flattened grey grass but the sky has large patches of blue between the grey bits. I say hello to the flower sellers, Marj and Ron, where Mum buys our fruit. Marj often gives me an extra red apple, or a perfect peach.

'How far d'ya get today darlin?'

'Only to the pond, but we saw a duck-fight. I think they're getting frisky because spring is coming. They were cavorting.'

'Cavortin' eh? Where does she get it from?' says Ron, picking out a dozen yellow roses for a short fat man with a long fur coat and piggy eyes.

They hoot with laughter at everything I say. Am I that amusing? Maybe I could do stand-up. There can't be many teenage comedians. I'd be a big hit.

Ron presents me with a red carnation. I do like him, even if he has only got three teeth.

Summer is meeting us at an ice-cream parlour in Hampstead. I wonder if she's changed? We see her before she sees us. She's talking on a mobile phone. She has two other girls with her, also talking on their phones. They look so silly, all talking to someone else, not to each other. They wear identical trainers and puffer jackets with fake-fur lined hoods. I have on my old Berlin parka, jeans, red Doc Martens and the England cricket cap Alistair gave me.

'Am I allowed to hug you?'

She looks like she'd rather not.

'Try.' We hug and jump up and down and squeal. We share the same birthday, 11th August, but she looks like fourteen rather than twelve and I look eleven at the most.

'Oh, Gussie, you look so well! Your cheeks are rosy. Your hair!' I forgot she hadn't seen my short spikes.

'Thanks, yeah, I feel great.'

'This is India and this is Sahara.' Is this an introduction or a geography lesson?

'What was the operation like?'

'Does it hurt?'

'Only when I laugh.'

'Have you got a big scar?'

'You look so well! You really do.'

I know I look a freak, with my cheeks puffed out from the steroids.

'What's your mobile number? You don't have a mobile?'

She wants to know all about our new home in Cornwall and promises that this year she will definitely come and stay. Mum goes shopping while we eat huge ices and when she comes back Mum pays. She's bought me a grey sweatshirt hoodie, sweatpants, socks and a long-sleeved grey T-shirt. So cool.

The three girls spend most of their time talking on their mobiles. They're catching a bus to Camden Lock and I'm invited, but I'm not sure. I worry that someone might bump into me. My incision scar is healing, but still weeps in places and is sore inside, as my entire breastbone was lifted up. I can see Mum's relieved when I decide not to go.

'Goodbye then, Gussie, see ya.'

Summer used to be my best friend, but somehow I have the feeling this is the last I'll see of her.

Mum takes my arm and we walk back through well-heeled crowds. (A foot metaphor: I collect them – 'footloose and fancy-free'; 'too big for his boots' – that sort of thing.) I am 'following in my paternal great-grandfather's footsteps', in that he was a famous photographer and I am learning how to make photographs. Mum says Daddy is 'a heel'. Not sure where that comes from. The lowest part of a body, perhaps. She certainly doesn't mean it kindly. I'm not 'head over heels' in love with Brett, but I do like him lots.

Must stop this line of thought.

I could get obsessed.

'Would you like a mobile phone?' Mum asks.

'Don't need one, thanks.' (Just thought of another – Charlie 'walks all over me' – literally and metaphorically.) 'Will my face look like my own face ever again?'

'Of course it will, Gussie. The swelling is only temporary, you know that.'

'Yeah, I suppose. Do you think Summer's pretty, Mum?' I know she is, don't know why I asked.

'She's pretty, darling. And you're extraordinary and interesting and gamine and elfin.'

'I think I'd rather be pretty.'

'It has its drawbacks.'

'How do you mean?'

'Sometimes other girls hate you and you have to be extra nice to your friends or they get jealous. And men are scared of pretty women. Anyway, your face is much more attractive than hers, don't you worry.'

'Really?'

'Yes. Summer's face isn't memorable, whereas yours is.'

'That's all right then,' I say and try to move along looking interesting and memorable. Come to think of it, some of my favourite actresses have interesting faces:

Bette Davis
Katherine Hepburn
Audrey Hepburn (I don't think they are related)
Lauren Bacall
Ingrid Bergman
Geena Davis
Meryl Streep
Helen Mirren
Helen Hunt

Daddy's favourites are:

Grace Kelly
Fay Ray (the one with a good scream in the original *King Kong*)
Most French film actresses, especially Jeanne Moreau and Catherine Deneuve – so all the pretty ones, then, excepting Jeanne Moreau.

CHAPTER SEVEN

OBLIQUELY—SLANTING; NEITHER PERPENDICULAR NOR PARALLEL; NOT AT RIGHT ANGLES: NOT PARALLEL TO AN AXIS

ECLECTIC—SELECTING OR BORROWING; CHOOSING THE BEST OF EVERYTHING; BROAD, THE OPPOSITE OF EXCLUSIVE; ONE WHO SELECTS OPINIONS FROM DIFFERENT SYSTEMS

ARDUOUS—STEEP, DIFFICULT TO CLIMB; DIFFICULT TO ACCOMPLISH; LABORIOUS

THREE NEW WORDS to use today – challenging my powers of memory as well as invention.

I am making photos of my father's flat. It's sparsely furnished, which is good: I don't have to move heavy stuff out the way, only our clothes and books. The low winter light falls obliquely through the slatted blinds across the pale wood floor. I am using black and white film, 400 ASA, on a tripod, Daddy's, of course. Another view is of his bed, the black mosquito net, classy, and the white flimsy muslin curtain blowing at the window. Very Hollywood, very Daddy.

When Alistair came up last time he brought me the tape-recorder he gave me for Christmas and several books I'd asked him for, and my binoculars, which I had forgotten to ask for, but he thought I might need them. He also brought a copy of the *St Ives Times and Echo* which has photos of the New Year's Eve celebrations – everyone in fancy dress. I do like that word – fancy. It sounds like what it means, special, unusual. I am front-page news! 'Augusta Stevens, aged 12, of St Ives, has received a new heart and lungs in a heroic, ten-hour operation on the last Boxing Day of the Twentieth Century.' I'm famous.

Daddy doesn't really have any proper novels here, only scripts and movie biographies and books on how to make movies. He used to like murder mysteries but I can't see any on his shelves. Mum and I have a more eclectic selection of reading matter – she's going through all the old Virago books – paperback novels by women who published in the early twentieth century and who had been out-of-print; writers like Kate O'Brian, Edith Wharton and Nina Bawden. She also reads modern novels.

This morning she left her bedroom book by the lavatory and I have been reading bits – *The Last Samurai,* by Helen de Witt. It's a novel about a genius child and it's very difficult and I can't understand most of it, as there's loads of maths and Japanese, and even Inuit, but I have learned one thing – a German phrase – *es regnete ununterbrochen,* which means – 'it rained uninterruptedly'. I must impress Mum with that. She can add it to the two German phrases she already knows.

Because I have missed so much school over the last few years, I have been educating myself. I read anything and everything I can get my hands on, especially books on nature. I spend my pocket-money on second-hand nature books. You can find really cheap ones at fleamarkets and car boot sales. I love WH Hudson on birds and nature and Fabre's *Insects* and White's *Natural History of Selborne*. Personal experiences of naturalists are much more interesting than purely scientific accounts.

I'm rereading *Jennie* by Paul Gallico, one of my all-time favourite novels. It's about a little boy who has an accident and wakes up to find he has turned into a cat. A stray cat, Jennie, has to teach him how to survive in London and how to behave like a cat, as he still thinks like a boy. It's the book that made me realise that I hadn't been seeing our cats properly. It taught me how to watch them, notice their habits and the way they live. In fact, it taught me to observe not only my cats but also other animals, including birds, insects and humans.

Alistair put up two birdfeeders in Daddy's garden. He's hung them from the skeletal branches of a copper beech, and Mum fills them with peanuts and sunflower seeds. It still hurts me to lift my arms above my head.

There weren't many birds around when we first arrived here, but now there are lots – sparrows, starlings, blackbirds, greenfinch, tits, and a robin. I have decided to try to tame the robin. You have to have mealworms though, so we'll have to find a pet shop.

I find one in the *Yellow Pages* and nag Mum until she drives me there.

'Can't we get Daddy some tropical fish? These blue and yellow ones would look so cool in his flat.' She ignores me; it's a tactic she's developed for not arguing. It usually works. 'Oh Mum, what about a terrapin?'

'A piranha would be good. With a Bit of Luck it Might Bite Him.' She's still bitter, I'm afraid.

We go home with a carton full of mealworms in a bed of bran. It says in the leaflet they are the larval form of the mealworm beetle, of the order of Coleoptera. They are about 2.5 cm, like the inchworm, and are mostly sold as bait to fishermen or for caged birds. Commercial mealworm growers incorporate a juvenile hormone into the feeding process, which keeps the mealworm in a larval stage and makes them bigger. We humans can't leave anything alone.

This is how the mealworm beetle mates: first the male chases the female until she gives up. The male then mounts her and curls his *aedagus* underneath him and inserts it into her genital tract. (I used to think genitals were called gentles.)

Once the male has inserted himself, he injects her with semen. In a matter of days the female will burrow into soft ground and lay between 70 and 100 eggs. After 4–11 days tiny mealworms start writhing around. During the larval stage the mealworms repeatedly shed their skin – about 10–14 times altogether. On its last shedding the mealworm loses its skin and then curls up into its pupal form, where it remains for between 6–30 days, depending on the temperature. It starts off creamy white and changes slowly to brown. (Another colour for my colour chart – Mealworm Pupa White.) Then they hatch as beetles, starting off as white and gradually turning brown, at which time they become sexually active and find a mate. And it all begins again.

I am at the pupa stage, waiting for my real life to begin, between a grub and a butterfly or moth, or maybe a mealworm beetle. Except that I mustn't think that way. Life is now, and I must live it.

One day someone will rename the inchworm the 2.5 cm worm.

I start off my robin-taming programme by putting a few mealworms in a shallow yoghurt pot lid on the ground near the back door, where Mr Robin often finds our leftover breadcrumbs. I put soggy breadcrumbs out there as well.

The first day, it rains hard and the worms are washed out onto the patio and I don't know what becomes of them. I think a thrush or blackbird might have found them when I wasn't looking. Today it's dry. I try again, standing by the door where the birds can see me. Mr Robin can't believe his luck and sings beautifully from the copper beech. I think he is saying thank you. I go out and crouch, having refilled the lid. After a few minutes the robin appears a few feet from me and nips quickly onto the lid where he picks up a worm or two and flies off. He's soon back, but this time I have put the worm-filled lid on the palm of my hand, the back of my hand flat on the ground. It's a rather uncomfortable position for me to hold, but he soon hops across to my hand, stands on my fingertips and eats from the lid. I hold my breath and gaze at his brick red breast feathers, his black beak and bead-like eyes. I cannot feel him on my fingers, he is so light.

He's away. Flown. I try again, on and off for an hour, but he hasn't returned. Maybe he's full and has other things on his mind, like finding a mate and defending his territory – Dad's back garden and the next one or two. I can hear him singing a long way off – a lilting sweet melody, like a woodland waterfall. I'll try again tomorrow. The wind chills me and I go inside and curl up on the sofa with a duvet, a hot water bottle and my book. I still sleep lots. It's an after-effect of the anaesthetic but I don't like sleeping in the daytime as I usually have bad dreams.

The next part of robin-taming means I have to put the mealworms directly into my palm, flatten my hand on the tiles and wait for the bird to be tempted. He actually lands on my fingertips after about five excruciatingly uncomfortable, freezing minutes and takes the mealworms from my palm. I can't believe it. I'll have to continue doing this each day so he becomes completely tame. We need more mealworms. Mum is not pleased. We are already spending a fortune in the pet shop, what with the peanuts and sunflower seeds. She is doing sketches of me with the bird. I think she misses her art classes.

I miss my cats. I remember silly things about them – like when I found a brave harvest mouse leaping up to attack Charlie's nose. She must have just brought it into the house and had dropped it, like they do, to play with the poor thing before the kill. I got to her just as she had dropped it and instead of running to hide he actually tried to bite her. I managed to rescue the courageous little beastie and release him before the *coup de grâce*. (I am picking up various foreign phrases that might come in useful sometime.)

One day before my operation I heard a tiny rattle behind the desk. I pulled out the desk and found that there was a mouse trying to chew its way into a walnut shell, which I had thrown for the cats to chase. I couldn't get the mouse, though I opened the door in the hope that it might find its way out and I put a little heap of birdseed for it behind the chest. No cat in sight, of course.

That same night Flo brought me a lovely, live harvest mouse. I picked it up and managed to drop it again before I could open the door. So then we had two mice in the house. Hopefully they were both males or there'll be a whole army of them when we get home.

My cats always know what to do on a rainy day. Flo goes hunting – she always catches something when it rains, carries it inside and mews loudly. I have to rescue the creature and put it out, then dry Flo with a towel, which she loves. I hate it when I find half a mouse, or a whole dead one squashed flat. (Why do cats roll on their victims?) The other two cats find their favourite warm spots – a high shelf, a cushion on a stool, a blanket on my bed – curl up and go to sleep to dream of killing and cream. Then they'll suddenly decide they want a new place to make their nest and they'll settle there for a week or two, before they're off again on a search for the perfect bed. They are like nomads.

I think I'd like to be a nomad. I'd buy a campervan and drive it all over the world looking for a perfect beach facing the sunset, or a lakeside meadow where geese come in their thousands every year at the same time. It might get lonely, although I expect you'd meet lots of interesting people. I could travel to all the places in the world where people are cruel to cats and I could rescue them and set up a travelling hospital for cats in my van. Or birds, of course. I could do what the sisters who started the Mousehole Bird Sanctuary did and look after injured birds. Little children would bring them to me and I would feed them and care for them until they were well and then I'd set them free. Except, of course, that now I have to watch out for cryptococcal or something or other. But that's okay: I'll wear rubber gloves and a face-mask like a surgeon.

We are going out the main front door of the building for our walk today, and meet an elderly German gentleman. He's the tenant of the first floor flat. I've seen his name on the door and seen him walking down the road.

'*Guten Abend,* Herr Weinberger,' I say.

'*Guten Abend, Liebchen.*' He smiles and nods and goes off down the street towards the village tapping his long white stick while we go up the hill towards the Heath. He looks rather down-at-heel (another foot expression). I expect it's because he can't see very well. It must be a consolation if you have poor eyesight, not to bother with your appearance, not care if your socks don't match or your collar is frayed, or your buttons aren't done up right.

'Very impressive, Gussie. Where did you learn German?'

'A book.'

'Say something else.'

'*Es regnete ununterbrochen* – it rained uninterruptedly.'

Her mouth stays open for several seconds. Then she starts laughing and can't stop. I laugh too but it hurts and I have to hold my chest.

There's a biting wind on the Heath and we only stop long enough by the pond for me to make a few photographs of the fluffed up ducks and swans on the lake. I stride out like I used to do when I was little, before I became really ill. It's so good to be able to do things other twelve year olds can do. Before, I was breathless even if I only walked across the room.

I wonder if I can teach Daddy to feed my robin? He might really like to do that. It would be almost like having a pet.

There's a group of science students and their tutors doing an ecological study of part of the Heath, taking notes of every living thing, including plants. Not that there seems to be much living at the moment. They look cold even their hoodies and parkas, woolly hats and gloves. I would love to do something like that. Perhaps I could do a study of our little garden in St Ives. I'll do it in the summer holidays when everything is alive. It shouldn't take long: the garden measures about 4 by 5 metres. Maybe Brett would like to help? It would mean dividing the garden into small squares, which I could do with string and pegs. I'll have to keep the cats out of the way somehow. I bet there are dozens of insect species. Coleoptera (beetles), and Lepidoptera (butterflies and moths) and spiders – what is their scientific name? Have we any inchworms, I wonder? Perhaps I could suggest it as a project at school, when I go back – after Easter, I hope.

We get back to the flat just as Mr Weinberger arrives.

'Would you like to come and have a cup of tea with me, *Liebchen,* with your *Mutti*?' And to Mum he says, 'I have some rather good single malt whisky if you would prefer, my dear, to warm you?'

'Sorry, Herr Weinberger, *Ich müss nach Hause gehen.*'

'Another time, thank you, Mr Weinberger, Gussie needs to rest now.'

I like the name *Mutti*. It's a prettier word than mother or mum.

The willows on the Heath greening up. Keats Grove is decorated with blossom in all the front gardens. It has been sunny and warm in Daddy's patio and Mr Robin has come to my hand twice today. He looks at me with his beady black eye, takes the mealworms and flies to the next garden. He's warbling. It sounds like a trickling stream of water or tiny bells. I wonder if I could tame any other birds?

I've found a second-hand book called *Birds as Individuals* by Len Howard – Len was a woman who allowed wild birds into her home to roost and they trusted her. (I thought Len was a man's name. Perhaps she wanted to be a man.) She was a sort of female Saint Sebastian. She recognised individual birds and even their facial expressions, and noted bird behaviour.

Sep 26th: Yet another couple of robins are pressing on west Robin and trying to get near the cottage via macrocarpus-tree and surrounding lawn. Four robins are now disputing this tree. From 3.30 until 5 p.m. a chase goes on, round and round the tree and its neighbouring apple-tree on the south-west. Dobs is furious; he sings incessantly with loud emphasis, often flying to the top of the bird-table to display, red-hot anger gleaming from his eyes. His head is enlarged, his body seems shrunken and his figure deformed. He is too agitated by this influx of Robins to take food offered him, he fears to stop singing or displaying for one moment, even to feed... For many hours the flutter of Robin wings is heard, hitting against the leaves as they dash headlong in and out, round and through the leaves. Dobs does not enter the chase but sings continuously from the bird-table, with flashing eyes and alarming contortions of his usually attractive form; also, he now resorts to the splutter-note, which had not hitherto demeaned his song.

In the book are photographs of a blue tit sitting on her finger as she draws, great tits perched on her shoulders and on her desk as she works at a typewriter. I wish I had known her. What was her secret? How did she get birds to accept her? She often mentions the facial expressions of birds. I know my cats' expressions well. I can tell if Flo is contented or mad. Charlie's always happy. She's a smiler. If she comes to me in the night, her eyes are black and round and she tiptoes. In the morning she's more likely to leap onto the bed, tail up high, mouth curved in a smile of pleasure. Rambo is the easiest cat to read. His tabby face is very expressive. He frowns, smiles, is worried, anxious, terrified – that more than anything else, he's such a wuss. Flo's emotions are complex. She shows disapproval very obviously: she glares mostly. If she's suddenly in need of affection she'll drool and look cross-eyed and stupid. I do miss my cats.

It's warm enough today to sit in the garden in the shelter of the wall for a little while. Daddy has these posh canvas deckchairs in a shed and we've got them out, but a small brown spider with a black head has laid its eggs on the seat of one of them. When I open the chair she pops out of her nest ready to defend her brood. I can't find her in my spider books. Maybe she is a rarity, a new spider, not described before. I could have a spider named after me: *Arachnida Gussii*.

> *Little Miss Muffet sat on a tuffet*
> *Eating her curds and whey.*
> *There came a big spider*
> *Who sat down beside her*
> *And frightened Miss Muffet away*

I don't know who wrote that – anon, I expect. She wrote lots of nursery rhymes.

Miss Muffet was the daughter of a spider expert – Reverend Thomas Muffet. When she was ill he made her eat crushed spiders as a cure. No wonder she was frightened of spiders. But most humans feel the same way. We spent a winter in the Seychelles when I was about nine. We had had a terrifying flight in a very small plane from a smaller island back to Mahe in a thunderstorm one evening. I walked into my bedroom, desperate for rest, and saw a hairy spider as big as Mum's hand on the back of the door. I jumped on the bed and screamed. Mum followed me in and screamed too. We bounced on the bed hugging each other like idiots for a few minutes; then she dragged me out, trying not to disturb the killer spider. We went to the cottage next door where a German family was staying. We needed help. Unfortunately they misunderstood our problem. Instead of removing the tarantula, they sprayed it with some awful slow-acting insecticide and it staggered around for an hour before dying. Worse, they found a whole family of them behind the wardrobe and killed them too. I still feel guilty when I think of it. I am quite brave about them now, well, braver than Mum (*Mutti*). I do the spider catching in our house. The ones we find in the bath are male house spiders, *Tegenaria domestica*, who have fallen in while looking for a mate. They can't climb out because they have no gripping tufts of hair on their feet to climb the shiny surface. Maybe Alistair will be her hero from now on. I hope so; it will relieve me of the arduous task.

There's one other tree in Daddy's garden. It's a Black Mulberry. Perhaps he could import some silkworms and start manufacturing silk. They prefer White Mulberry leaves, though.

We had some silk worms at school once. They're the caterpillar of *Bombyx mori* – a moth. Someone came to the school and showed us how they live. The silk actually comes from the cocoon. The larva constructs its cocoon from a single strand of silk, laid down in a figure-of-eight motion. When the adult moth emerges it breaks through the silk, damaging the strand. This makes it unusable, as the silk can't be unwound, so silk manufacturers kill the pupa before the moth inside leaves its cocoon. They place them in hot-air dryers, which dessicates them so the pupae will not putrefy in stored cocoons.

I don't imagine they feel any pain – I do hope not. But if you think about it it's a bit like mass abortion. There are hardly any silk worms in the wild, but there must be some as there is such a thing as wild silk. Mankind has farmed them for thousands of years.

Mum has lots of silk: shirts and silk scarves. I better tell her not to buy more unless it's wild and free range.

As soon as we get settled in the garden the sun disappears and it's winter again. But it was a promise of sunny times to come.

Mum and I are invited to Herr Weinberger's flat. There is a wall of shelves full of brightly coloured pottery figures, but no books at all. I look at the names on the base of two figures on horses – Havelock and Campbell, and seated figures of Queen Victoria and Prince Albert.

After he died, Victoria wore mourning black for the rest of her life. I remember that from a radio programme. I like Radio Four, which *Mutti* listens to most of the time. There's lots of talking on it, debates, stories, plays – *Woman's Hour* and the *Today* programme. *Mutti* shouts at one of the presenters sometimes, telling him to shut up so she can hear what the interviewee has to say. I can't concentrate on things in the morning until I've had all my medicines and done my health checks. We have a home spirometry kit: I have to blow really hard and it measures my breathing, which I record in a special notebook with my temperature and weight and what drugs I take and when. If I have a sudden weight loss, I have to phone the hospital in case it's a sign of some major problem – like rejection.

'Do you like my pottery figures, Gussie?'

'What are they, Herr Weinberger?'

'They are Victorian. Decorated by children, mostly. They were made as souvenirs of popular figures – people in the news – generals, celebrities and royalty.'

'Like posters of pop musicians?'

'Yes, Gussie, similar. People collected figures of people they admired. This one is Jenny Lind, a very famous singer in her day.'

'Are they German?'

'No, no, English. Staffordshire pottery. I love English things, not German, and I love Scottish things – their single malt whiskies, at least.' He laughs at his own little joke. 'Try this ten year old cask-made Laphroaig, my dear.'

He pours a drink for Mum and I have apple juice. Mum murmurs her appreciation. He asks about my treatment and Mum tells him, but I don't want to talk about my illness or my operation, it's boring.

'What did you do before you were old, Herr Weinberger?' I ask. He laughs.

'Gussie, that's not polite.' Mum sighs loudly. 'I'm sorry, Herr Weinberger.'

'No, no, don't worry, she has an enquiring mind, *das ist zehr gut*. I was a jeweller in Hatton Garden.'

'A jeweller? Did you make brooches and necklaces?'

'Yes, and I worked with diamonds. I designed and made diamond rings, brooches, necklaces and that sort of thing. I worked with precious stones, silver, gold and platinum until my eyes became too weary.'

When we leave, he says we must return. I think he's lonely. I wonder if he talks to his Staffordshire figures. He looks surprisingly well dressed and scrubbed today.

CHAPTER EIGHT

THE THING ABOUT being in hospital was – people looked after me. I was the centre of attention, the star. Everyone was striving to keep me alive, or that's what it felt like. I was special; I was important. And why were they all trying to save me? Why did I survive? Am I here for a reason? Are we all alive simply to reproduce for the survival of the species? I suspect we are but I would like to do something useful or wonderful with my new life. I'm like the Tin Man in *The Wizard of Oz*, who had no heart until Dorothy helped him to get one. Mr Sami is my Dorothy. But what could I do? Perhaps become a doctor or a nurse? Or encourage people to become organ donors? Or a writer? A poet? I think I might be a poet. Yes, a poet. For now anyway.

Missing Them

I miss the meow and prrup
The jumping up onto my lap,
The floating fur, the chirrup and purr
The cold pink nose, the curling tail
The gift of mouse, shrew and vole.
I miss the chase the pounce the kill.

Mum has been acting oddly. When she's not organising my drugs, preparing meals, or spending ages in the bathroom, she's watching the telly, turning up the volume and then dozing off, head thrown back, mouth open, snoring loudly, like an old woman. She's fifty-three so I suppose she is fairly old. If only she could see herself. I make a photo of her – I could use it as blackmail. When she's awake she shouts at the telly or talks to herself, wherever she is, bathroom, kitchen, sitting room, and I assume she's talking to me, but she isn't. I worry about her. Is she losing her marbles?

'Come on *Mutti*, I'm taking you out.'

'I don't want to go out. I was awake all night. I want to listen to *Woman's Hour*.'

'What about my walk?'

'What about it?'

'Well, I have to exercise.'

'Well, go on then, exercise.'

'I can't go on my own. What about the perverts?'

'What perverts? Have we ever met any perverts?'

'Well, no…'

'Oh, go on Guss, you'll be all right. Give it a try.'

I have never been out on my own in London, I realise; in Cornwall, yes, but here? No. I always went to school by car with Mum or bus with friends.

I suppose the worst that can happen is that some poor sick man will expose himself to me. Ohmygod, I hope that doesn't happen. I've survived a heart and lung transplant; I can surely survive a walk on the Heath.

'I'll be back,' I say in my best Arnold Schwarzenegger *Terminator* voice.

The Heath is icy and bleak, joggers are scarlet with cold even though it's meant to be spring. The dog-walkers hurry along, yanking the leads when their pugs and poodles stop to sniff each other's bums. Isn't it odd that humans have pets? Some humans. It's not like the pets are doing a job – like sheep dogs or gun dogs; they don't clean our skins like small fish do for whales and sharks, or eat parasites from cattle like cowbirds. We keep them because we enjoy their company. We groom *them,* not the other way round. It's very strange that we like having animals around – especially dogs, as most of the dogs I've met smell pretty awful if they aren't bathed regularly. Not like my cats, who smell of leaves and earth. And their breath is gross too – dogs, I mean. One of my grandma's friends used to have an old spaniel. I couldn't sit on her carpet because it smelled so bad. Like… like… well, like smelly old dog.

In Darwin, Australia, some people buy baby crocodiles as pets for Christmas presents. Brett told me that. More macho than Rottweilers or Staffordshire pit bull terriers apparently. Crocodiles, not Brett, though he is pretty macho.

The willows are green with new growth but no other trees have signs of life, apart from skulking crows, who hunch their black shoulders like coffin bearers and peer down on me as if they are measuring me. Swans drift, heads tucked under wings.

I must at least have a little adventure, now I'm on my own. But there's no prince on a white stallion, no unicorns or dragons, no perverts even.

'Herr Weinberger! *Guten Abend.*'

'*Guten Tag, Liebchen.* It is Augusta, *nicht war?*'

He pronounces my name 'owgoosta', which sounds very strange.

'*Ya, aber ich müss nacht Hause gehen.*' I only say this to impress him. It means but I have to go home now.

'Oh, what a shame, can't you walk with me for a while?'

'Well, okay, just for a little while.'

I stare at his stick and the thick lenses of his specs.

'Are you completely blind, Herr Weinberger?'

'I don't see very well. But I see you have a camera – a Leica, *nicht war?*'

'Yes. Daddy lent it to me.'

'I too have one of these. *Zehr gut* this camera. It is made in Germany.'

'I thought you didn't like German things, Herr Weinberger.'

'That is right. Yes, yes, usually, but the German camera, it is *zehr gut*.'

'My great-grandfather was a famous photographer. His name was Amos Hartley Stevens. Maybe you've heard of him?

'*Nein, nein,* I do not know this name. But famous? *Ach, Liebchen.* Then you maybe will be famous also. It will be in your blood, so?'

'Maybe. I really must go home now, though, before I get chilled.'

'Off you go, my dear, don't you worry about me.'

He coughs and sniffs. Maybe because his sight isn't good his sense of smell is more developed. That happens sometimes. One sense becomes stronger when others are weak.

I wonder how old he is and if he was an enemy soldier in the Second World War. And now we are friends – or friendly. If generals and colonels, admirals and politicians fought *each other* when they declared war, instead of getting young soldiers to fight their wars for them, maybe the world would be a better place, though it would be more crowded.

Maybe Nature has made humans warlike and bloodthirsty as a built-in way of keeping down the world's population.

He hasn't the right shape for a soldier – he's small and thin. He wears a holey tweed coat, a tatty fur hat and scarf and smells of mothballs and lemony cologne. His socks are tucked into his boots.

He coughs.

'Yes, I better get back. Bye.'

'*Auf Wiedersehen, Liebchen.*'

I walk through frosty leaves that crackle and crunch under my Doc Martens. There is a boy sitting on a rug in the doorway of a closed deli. He looks about fifteen, red-eyed, skinny and spotty, wrapped in a woollen blanket. I go into the café next door, buy a take-away hot chocolate and a melted cheese and tomato baguette. It takes practically all of my pocket money.

'Here.'

He looks astonished and turns red.

I take out the last pound coin from my pocket and give it to him.

'What's this?' Bridget's gold star lies twinkling in his grubby hand.

'Oh, that's mine – a friend gave it to me for luck.' I take it from him and walk quickly away.

'Thanks,' he calls.

I turn and wave. Mum would be proud of me. She doesn't usually give money to homeless people but she tries to help them in practical ways. Perhaps I should have given him something else – my cap or scarf? But the cap is an official England cricket cap, and I know Alistair would be upset if I gave it away. Also, Mum says you lose most of your heat through the top of your head, and I need the scarf to keep my chest warm.

Perhaps I'll take him one of Mum's scarves. She's got lots. She has a thing about shoes, scarves and bags. And dresses, and jackets and coats, jumpers, jeans and skirts. I can't see the attraction, but she says I will, soon.

I feel guilty now. I should have left him the gold star. He needs more luck than me. He looked disappointed when I took it back.

I wish I had asked Alistair to bring me my computer, but I

suppose it would be a bit much to ask. Also, I need someone to teach me how to use it.

We're at the swimming pool for Mum's first aqua-fit class. She says she is becoming a fat slug, feels bloody awful, her back hurts and she needs to boost her energy levels. I would have liked to join in but I am not allowed to use swimming pools for reasons beyond my comprehension. More germs I suppose.

Elsa, South African, big but no fat on her, though she is not slim, is the teacher. 'Shame' – she says as Mum explains about my operation and why I cannot get into the water. Mum wants to look like her. She says her buttocks used to look like that, before she had me.

There are ten women. The air is tropically warm, like it was in Kenya. It's a small swimming pool but the same depth water throughout. They talk and laugh above loud taped music, all old stuff. They all know the words, and sing along to Tom Jones, The Beach Boys, Elvis Presley, the Beatles.

I take a few photos of them cavorting in the water singing 'Lucy in the Sky with Diamonds'. Cavorting – I like that word. The Leica makes a very soft whisper when I open the shutter, not like my Nikkormat, which clicks.

They should be wearing flowery swim-caps, then they would look like a hydrangea bush. But they do look as if they are enjoying themselves. I imagine Mum diving into the middle of the chorus of swimmers like Esther Williams in *Million Dollar Mermaid*. I do love classic movies, especially musicals. Fred Astaire and Ginger Rogers. And *The Thin Man* – that funny dog.

Mum goes in the jacuzzi afterwards. She likes the blasts of water on her back. When she gets out of the water she says she can feel how heavy she is, the force of gravity. (I always think that when Mum is seriously cross with me, *I* feel the force of her gravity.)

Afterwards, I have a hot chocolate, which isn't that hot, but I like the sprinkles of chocolate on the top. Mum has a decaf black coffee and a large piece of carrot cake at the café. Having felt briefly smug, she says, she now feels guilty. The other ladies are gathered round and chatting. One is with her daughter, who looks about seventy, so goodness knows how old she is. She smiles at me and asks why I didn't join in the class.

'I'm recovering from a heart and lung transplant,' I say.

'My goodness, are you really? I didn't know they did such things.'

'Yes, she isn't allowed in swimming pools in case of infection.'

'What a shame! Perhaps when you are better?'

'No, I can never ever go into a swimming pool ever again.'

'How sad!'

'I think you can after a year, Gussie,' says Mum.

'Oh, that's good news.'

However, it doesn't sound nearly so dramatic.

The old lady's name is Alice and she is eighty-nine. She has done loads of things in her life – like designing hats for a fashion house, and she was in the Women's Air Force in the war.

I didn't like to ask which war.

She says she enjoys the aqua-fit classes even though she can't do many of the exercises and gets very bored at home, and I suggest she writes down her life story for her family. I wish my grandparents had done that. I tell her she better do it quickly before she dies or becomes unable to see or use her hands or something. I get hustled off home by Mum before

I've finished telling Alice how to spend the rest of her life.

'Gussie, you really mustn't be so fierce with people.'

A parcel and card (photo of baby seal) from Brett:

Hi Guss,
Howyadooin? Hope you are feeling better. I've finished
Hitchhiker's Guide to the Galaxy. *It's beauty. 'Life?*
Don't talk to me about life.' Marvin the robot's line,
not mine. I recommend it. It's full of crazy ideas and
happenings. I won't spoil it for you.
See ya,
Brett x

He's sent me the book. Daddy used to be mad on it too. He was always quoting stuff from it. Like, 'DON'T PANIC.'

I do like getting letters. Hearing someone's voice on the telephone is good but you can't take it out and look at it again like you can a letter.

I write back straight away and tell him about Mr Robin, the ducks and other birds on the Heath and say I am still birding when I can. I don't mention the streptawhatever. I don't want to be abnormal, I want to be treated as if I am the same as everyone else.

I have a pile of nature books to read. I get a feeling of security and anticipation having a pile of unread books next to my bed. I also like to reread favourites – like the *Just William* books and *Swallows and Amazons.*

Mum is invited for a drink at Herr Weinberger's flat. I don't go; I'm too busy reading.

When she comes downstairs I see she has been crying.

'What's the matter Mum? Aren't you happy now I've had my transplant?'

She hugs me to her, being careful of my scar.

'Oh, darling, of course I'm happy, very happy, over the moon.' She has a red nose. 'Willy and I were talking about evil.' She sniffs loudly.

'Evil?'

'Yes. Herr Weinberger's Jewish, you know. He's the only survivor in his family. He escaped from Germany before the war. His parents and brothers, aunts and uncles were all killed by the Nazis.'

'Oh, I see.'

'Do you remember when we were in Kenya, finding coral together on the beach?'

'No.'

'Tiny red fragments with a hole in. We made necklaces from them.'

'I remember a red necklace. It was scratchy.'

'A huge empty beach and a white man in swimming trunks suddenly walked between us, separating us. It was as if we didn't exist. He had a scar from his head right down through one blind eye and down to his chin. He only had one arm. The other one ended in a stump above the elbow.'

'No, I don't remember him.'

'He looked like someone who had seen and done terrible things. He looked evil.'

'What did you do?'

'Grabbed you and took you back to the house. I never saw him again.'

'Maybe you imagined him?'

'No, he existed.' She is crying again and I am holding her around her waist.

CHAPTER NINE

LIFELINE—A ROPE FOR SAFEGUARDING OR SAVING LIFE; A VITAL LINE OF COMMUNICATION

WHAT I DO remember of Africa, the first winter there, is all the cripples in Mombasa. A man with no legs trundling himself along in the heavy traffic on a sort of square of wood with wheels, like a primitive skateboard. People with no eyes or no arms, begging in the streets. Sweaty, half-naked men striding along with mattresses or huge bunches of bananas balanced on their heads. Bikes overloaded with people and heavy loads. Children smiling and waving. The smell of the meat market. Humidity and heat. Air-conditioning in the cinema and bank. The stink of a dead elephant on a bush track. Poachers had hacked out the tusks and the wrinkled skin had shrivelled onto its sad ribs. The vultures ignored us and just kept on tearing at the flesh. I can still smell it. And I remember vervet monkeys leaping from a sausage tree, hugging their babies to their chests. Huge butterflies flapping through the palms. Giant tortoises at the funny guest house along the beach, which was like a black and white Elizabethan cottage. Prints of Cornwall on the walls. The scent of pepper and charcoal burning, sweet potatoes. Air like cotton wool.

I learned to swim in Africa: first with armbands in a pool, then by snorkelling over the reef and in the shallows of the lagoon. You wouldn't believe the fish I saw. They were like imaginary fish, not real, all colours and patterns. Puffer fish blown up like balloons were washed in dead on the beach. There were giant clams, lion fish, sea snakes, moray eels, orange and white striped clownfish hiding in the waving tentacles of sea anemones, that are poisonous to other fish but not to clownfish. We never saw a shark; there are lots there, but they stay outside the reef. So they said. Mum used to sit on the verandah teaching herself to type on her portable typewriter. I remember a black man called Zackariah, who cooked and cleaned for us.

It's warm enough today to sit outside again. The patio's a suntrap. Mum finds the sun screen – I have to have it on even in winter if the sun shines, and I put on my cricket hat. The deckchairs come out, but we still can't use the spider nursery. They've hatched, tiny cream babies, remaining inside the webby nest with their mother. Does she feed them at this stage, I wonder? Only one baby has braved the world outside the silken nest. It looks bigger than the others. The survivor. I don't think mother spider approves of exposing her babies to the bright light of day, so I close the deckchair again. When will they disperse? I had no idea spiders were such caring mothers, or that their eggs took so long to hatch, or that the spiderlings (I love that word) stay in the nest so long. Maybe they are sick babies, or premature, and need extra time in the nursery. Spiderlings often fly away on silk threads to avoid being eaten by their siblings.

Why is it I can never find the creature I am looking at in a reference book? They never look the same as they do in photos or illustrations. Are they all new discoveries? I'll have so many bugs named after me, I'll be as famous as Darwin.

We've run out of mealworms. Mum says they are too expensive, but Mr Robin comes to my hand anyway for wild birdseed. He is perfect, with his scarlet breast and black button eyes. He watches me as I watch him. What do birds think about people? Do they see us as flightless birds, with featherless wings? Or maybe they think our clothes are feathers? They might sit around on trees on the Heath watching us and admiring a red coat or a yellow hat or blue trousers and green shoes as we walk under them. We must be difficult to label: a juvenile, lesser-spotted, white-faced geek; a glossy, red-beaked shopper. I would be a juvenile, blue-capped, red-footed walker. Mum is a moulting magpie. No, that's cruel. She's a mature, black-capped female, caring for her one and only sickly fledgling. I'm lucky she hasn't thrown me out of the nest. Most creatures are pretty cruel when it comes to caring for sickly young, except elephants and some big cats. It's all part of Nature's survival of the fittest rule. People are much kinder to *their* unhealthy offspring, loving them just as much as their healthy babies.

My biopsies are going well, though I hate them. There's this awful feeling of uneven heart beat when the catheter is in there, which reminds me of how it was BT. No sign of more problems, touch wood. That's a silly superstition and I'm not superstitious, but anyway it can't do any harm to touch wood even if it doesn't do any good.

I feel that the hospital has become the main part of my life – a lifeline. I have more friends there than in the real world. Well, not friends exactly, but people I know and need, expert nurses and medics. Katy and Soo Yung, my transplant nurses; Dolores in physio, who always has a smile for me. She says she looks forward to having me to look after as I always make her laugh. I think it's the other way round – she makes me laugh. She thinks I always tell her something she doesn't know. She says I'm a clever clogs. Is that a good thing I wonder, or is she being ironic or sarcastic? It's another foot expression to add to my list.

My visits to hospital will soon go down to one every two weeks. Twelve weeks after the transplant they go down to monthly visits for six months, then two monthly – which means we'll have to travel from Cornwall quite often, but it also means I get to see Daddy more often.

I loathe the anti-fungal liquid I have to swallow, against thrush. (Why it's called thrush?) But apart from the occasional nausea and mood swing I feel stronger every day and my scar is nearly healed. There are only one or two places that are sore and still need dressings. My face is still puffy. I hope the cats recognise me when we go home. But I suppose my smell hasn't changed and that's how cats recognise people, as well as by their voice. Charlie always comes running when I call her name. But maybe the drugs I have to take are changing my body smell? When Mum has just applied hand cream or body lotion, Flo will flee from her in disgust. She has a more sensitive nose than the other two cats or she takes offence more than they do.

I'm worried about Mum. She spends more and more time in the bathroom, even in the night, and is very weepy. She can't still be worrying about evil?

CHAPTER TEN

'GUSSIE, GUSSIE, HELP! Help me!'

I wake from a dream where Mum's calling for me and I am stuck in mud and cannot move my legs. I need help but she's wanting help from me.

It isn't a dream.

'I'm coming, I'm coming.'

I open the bathroom door and find her slumped on the tiled floor. Her face is white. I slip on blood and save myself from falling by hanging on to the wash-basin. It jars my chest and hurts my ribs and scar.

'Get an ambulance, Gussie.'

I don't know what to do. Help her? Phone first and then help her?

'You're bleeding to death!'

'No, I'm not. Just get an ambulance. Now. Dial 999. Tell them, a haemorrhage.'

I leave her there, naked on the floor, and phone 999. Then I bring two large towels from the airing cupboard and put them around her. I've made bloody footprints all over the carpet.

She's very pale. She keeps fading away, losing consciousness, and I have to shout at her to come back to me.

'Please don't die, Mummy, don't die!'

I hold her cold hand.

I'm covered in blood. I sit on the floor with her and rub her hand in mine to warm her.

She looks bad. I want to get her address book so I can phone Daddy but I can't leave her in case she dies when I'm not there to hold her.

The doorbell rings.

The ambulance men gently tell me to stay out of the way while they examine Mum.

'Is she dead? She's not dead is she?'

'No, she's not dead.'

I explain about her fibroids. The blue light flashes through the window. It's raining hard. I pull on combat trousers, a sweatshirt. I'm still wearing pyjamas underneath. I grab the address book from the hall table – my hands are still covered in blood.

'You want to come along?' the tall one asks. They are strapping her onto a stretcher. She is wrapped in blankets, swaddled like a papoose. There's a mask over her face. It doesn't look like Mum. It's someone smaller, older, helpless.

'I'll get my coat.'

I put on the parka, cricket cap and scarf. It's cold. I remember the keys, lock the door and get in the back of the ambulance.

We are at the Accident and Emergency Unit within five minutes and Mummy is whisked away behind a curtain.

Mummy is now having an emergency operation and I am in a waiting room on my own. It has mustard-yellow walls and an acid green floor – enough to make anyone feel ill – and sagging chairs. There's a pay phone, so I phone Alistair but he's not answering, so I call Daddy and leave a message. I don't know what else to do. I am looking in Mum's address book to see if I can find the friends who came to supper. I only know their first names – Mimi and, and… I've forgotten *The French Connection*'s real name. Can't find them. I've read all the torn and grubby magazines and feel like I need a shower. They allow people to smoke in here; the ashtrays are full; it's smelly. I think it's a staff rest room. I suddenly see the convenience of a mobile phone. No one can reach me here, not that it would make any difference, since mobile phones aren't allowed in hospitals.

I really thought Mum was dying when I found her. All that blood. I'm still shaking. I wish I could wash my hands.

A night duty nurse told me to sit in here and she brought me a cup of tea. It's off the main Casualty waiting area. She said it would be safer for me here as it's full of drunks and overdoses in there and 'the language is not for young ears'.

I had no idea there was so much going on at two in the morning: a bearded man with a broken hand, and his girlfriend, who is looking pissed off and has a black eye; a smelly tramp, with a bloody foot, asleep; a druggy looking girl with a boy with long greasy hair. She has her hand covered by a bloody tea-towel. Another ambulance arrives and a wrapped body is wheeled into another cubicle. Groans and sobs come from behind curtains. Doctors and nurses in bloody gowns rush about looking harassed and exhausted. There's a lot of shouting and swearing. It's like *Mash* without the music and helicopters.

A doctor comes to see me and says I ought to go home and wait, as I can't see Mum until she's come round from the anaesthetic. She sends me home in a hospital car. I've told her there'll be someone there to look after me later this morning. It's not really a lie; Daddy will come when he hears what's happened. I don't think she really knew what else to do with me.

The driver sees me unlock the door of Daddy's flat and switch the light on before he drives off. It's cold in here; the central heating hasn't come on yet and I don't know how to do it. I put the radio on to keep me company, make a cup of hot milk and a hot water bottle. My pyjamas are covered in blood. I stuff them in the linen basket and find another pair.

I have a shower and go to bed. The sky is black and a strong wind rattles the windows and cries in the trees. I don't like the sounds the building makes – creaking and tapping as if ghosts are about; a eerie whistling through the letter box; a branch scraping against the window. At least I have Rena Wooflie to keep me company. I tell her not to worry, I'm here and she mustn't be scared. I wish Charlie and Flo and Rambo were purring in my ear and marching on my duvet, vying with each other for the warmest position. I hope Claire isn't getting flea-bites. An owl shrieks in the dark and I wonder what poor little victim has been caught. A screech owl call is a bad omen. I read that somewhere.

I can't wait any longer but it's only 6 a.m. Daddy's mobile is turned off. I don't know the Snow Queen's second name or address or telephone number. I try Alistair on his mobile phone.

'Gussie, what's the matter?'

'Oh Alistair…' I burst into tears.

Eventually he gets the story from me, but he can't come. He's in Bulgaria, at a conference. He'll be back on Thursday. It's Monday now.

'What shall I do?'

'Can you take all your drugs on your own? Take your temperature? Spirometry?'

'Yes, I think so. I've got a kit. Mum made a chart. It's in the kitchen. And I've got a book to fill in.' I sound stupid, but I do know what to do. The main thing is to remember to take the 10 o'clocks on an empty stomach. It's a drag but I'm used to it now. It's all about habit. Most things in life are about habit. Grandma used to say, if you remember every day to clean your teeth, bath or shower, clean your nails, blow your nose and wash behind your ears, you'll always be clean and decent without even thinking about it. And if you ask your small children always to say please and thank you and excuse me when they want to get past someone in the way, or they want to talk to someone who is already talking to someone else, they'll grow up with good manners. And good manners never did any one any harm, Grandma always said.

'Right. Well carry on and look after yourself, Gussie, I know you can do that. You're a sensible girl.' I sniff loudly. 'I'll come as soon as I can. Any problems, phone your hospital. Where's your father?'

'Don't know. I tried him last night but he wasn't answering.'

'Heavens to Murgatroyd! Did you leave a message?'

'Yes, I told him Mum was very ill and was having an operation. Oh, Alistair, will she be okay? She won't die, will she?'

'Of course not, Gussie, don't worry about her; she's in good hands. I'll phone the hospital in a moment and find out what's happening. Lots of women her age have to have a hysterectomy. She'll be fine.'

'But it was an emergency operation.'

'Yes, I know, I know. But she'll be fine. It's no big deal. Believe me.'

I do believe him, he always sounds so reassuring.

'Give me your father's telephone number and I'll get hold of him. And what's the neighbour's name? The old boy upstairs?'

After I put the phone down I burst into tears again, and produce a puddle of self-pity.

I phone the hospital but the line is busy. I phone Claire in Cornwall. She's horrified I'm on my own.

'Where's your father?'

I explain.

She says she will try and get him. I think I ought to wait for someone to phone me now. Daddy wouldn't have been able to get through to me as I've been talking for the last hour.

Ring ring. It's the front door.

'Herr Weinberger!' I burst into tears yet again. What is this? I'm usually quite brave. *True Grit* is what's needed in this situation. He heard the ambulance arrive in the night and assumed it was for me. Alistair has phoned him. He invites me to his flat, but I say I must stay by the phone in case Daddy rings.

'Oh yes, your father. He will come, of course. Oh, *Mein Gott*, the carpet!' He has brought some cake that he made himself. It has roasted sunflower seeds on top. 'I shall stay with you until he comes.'

'Oh, could you? Thank you.' When I have stopped blubbing I make us a pot of tea. Mr Robin comes to the patio window and begs for some cake. I open the door, hold the crumbs in my hand, and Mr Robin takes them neatly and eats.

'He likes your cake, Herr Weinberger,' I whisper.

'Call me Willy, my dear. Herr Weinberger makes me feel old.'

I laugh and Mr Robin flies off.

The phone rings.

'Daddy!'

'Gussie, I'll be right there. Give me an hour. Is Willy there?'

'Yes.'

'Good. See you ASAP. *Ciao*.'

I phone the hospital and after an age get put through to the right department. Mummy has had the operation and I can go to see her this evening.

'How is she?'

'As well as can be expected.'

What does that mean?

Fay phones and asks if she should come up to London but I explain that Daddy will be here soon. She tells me that my cats are settling in at the Darling's house, and have already learned not to chase the chickens, as the cockerel has had words with them. They are scared of the rabbits and ducks and stay out of their way too.

Oh I do miss Charlie and need her to cuddle. She always knows when I need sympathy.

The key turns in the front door. 'Daddy! Oh Daddy!' He gives me a big hug and when I have recovered myself, Herr Weinberger has gone. 'Will you stay with me, now, Daddy?'

'Of course I will, my little honeybun.'

After phoning the hospital, he clears up the bathroom – he says it's a scene from *Chainsaw Massacre*. Then he makes up a clean bed for himself on the sofa-bed. He's washed the bloody footprints from the wooden floor of the hall and has phoned for a cleaner to come to get it off the sitting room carpet. He even starts the washing machine. I had no idea he could be so domesticated.

'Right, Gussie, I'm taking you out for a coffee.'

'I don't drink coffee.'

'Hot chocolate then.'

'You're on. *Breakfast at Tiffany's*?'

In the end we have breakfast and lunch – brunch – in a café. This is the longest time I've spent with my father since my parents split up. And he hasn't got a girlfriend with him: he's all mine. He gets me to tell him about how I feel and how many drugs I have to take each day. I am confident I can manage my own drug regime now and he seems to think I can.

'How did a girl like you get to be a girl like you?'

He's Cary Grant and I'm Eva Marie Saint in *North by Northwest*.

I tell him all about his Cornish family – Aunt Fay, her son Moss, Claire – Moss's wife, and their children Phaedra, Troy and Gabriel; their home that Moss built, and garden full of livestock and vegetables; Great Aunt Fay's cabin and her fluffy cat.

'You must come to Cornwall and meet them Daddy, they are so nice, you'd love them, really you would.'

'Yes, I'll get to meet them some time, I'm sure.'

'How come you didn't know about your grandfather being a famous photographer?'

'I dunno, Guss, I'm just not into family history, that's all. But come to think of it, there's a load of stuff in a box somewhere. I'll dig it out.'

'Stuff? What sort of stuff?'

'Oh you know, my parents' stuff. I chucked most of it but there're a few bits left. We'll have a look when I remember where I put it.'

'Can we do it today?'

'Yeah, yeah, later.'

'Daddy, will Mum need looking after when she comes out of hospital? Will we have to stay in London? When will we be able to go back to Cornwall?'

'I haven't the faintest idea. We'll find out from the doctors. What's happening with the boyfriend? Thought he was here.'

'Alistair?'

'Yeah, the dour Scot.'

'What's dour?'

'Oh, you know, boring, straight, glum.

'He'll be back on Thursday. He's in Bulgaria.' Why didn't

I defend Alistair? I feel angry with myself and with Daddy. I should have said, 'If you mean he's serious and honest and trustworthy, yes, he is straight and he's kind actually and I think Mummy loves him. And he's not boring and I like him very much.' But I said nothing.

Daddy phones the girlfriend and I can't help overhearing, even though he gets up and walks around. He's telling her to cool it, and be reasonable. I think she might be jealous. '*Ciao*,' he says and puts his mobile phone in his pocket. I wish he wouldn't say '*Ciao*'. It sounds so... so false. He's not Italian.

'Daddy, are you going to look for the box of stuff?'

'I suppose so. It might be in the cupboard under the stairs.'

It is: a dusty cobwebby cardboard box. He hauls it out, wipes it with a damp cloth and we sit on the floor to open it. It's like Christmas.

Something big and bulky in cotton cloth. Daddy unwraps a large camera – a Rolleiflex.

'A twin lens reflex, Guss, see – two lenses. Invented in 1928 – German.'

'Is this what your grandfather used?'

'I suppose it must be. Don't remember my old man doing any photography.'

'So, it's the famous Amos Hartley Stevens' camera?'

'Yep, could be.'

'Does it still work? Can you still get film for it?'

'I think so. There's a whizz-kid at the archive. I'll ask him to check it over.'

We rummage deeper and find a pile of square card boxes, tied with string. Inside each one is a pile of film negatives 2¼ x 2¼ inches, separated by brown tissue paper. Holding them up to the light, we see black and white negative images of St

Ives harbour and the town, boats and gulls and people.

'I had no idea,' says Daddy, shaking his head. 'This is quite a find.'

'What will you do with them?'

'Get them printed. We'll see how good they are then.'

He parcels them up carefully back in the boxes, which are dated – 1928, 1929, 1930, 1931, 1932. Five years' work by a famous Cornish photographer, hidden in Daddy's cupboard (the work, not the photographer).

Daddy's brought his laptop with him. It's so amazing. I watch him type.

'Daddy, could you give me a lesson in computers please?'

'Sure. Not now, though. I have some catching up to do.'

Brett has a computer and I'm sure he'll help me when I get home.

In the evening after a snack supper and my drugs regime we walk to the Royal Free Hospital. It's only around the corner. We have a bag of stuff for Mum – soap, face cream, toothbrush, toothpaste, moisturiser, dressing gown.

'Oh, I didn't bring flowers!' I say, and then remember that flowers aren't allowed in hospital wards any more. The flower seller outside has lost his main customers. Mum would have loved some sunflowers. They're her favourites after cornflowers, sweet peas and marigolds.

Mum is lying in bed wearing a hospital gown. She looks pale and not at all pretty, not even interesting and memorable. She gives me a weak smile and I kiss her cheek. Daddy does too.

'Mummy, I thought you were going to die.'

She looks too frail to hug. I am crying again.

'Oh Gussie, darling, you were so wonderful. Don't cry

now. I'm much better than I was last night,' she says, 'and about a stone lighter.'

'Have you got a big scar?'

'Not as big as yours.'

'That's all right then. We'll compare them later.' I say, wiping my face with my sleeve, and she smiles.

'I'll show you mine if you show me yours,' she says. Then to Daddy, 'It's good of you to come.'

'Not at all, not at all.'

'You realise I'm not allowed to lift anything heavier than a half-full kettle for six weeks. Won't be able to drive, can't hoover, can't hang up the washing. Can't do a bloody thing.'

She's upset. Mum hates being dependent, she prefers to be in charge. Daddy says she's a control freak.

'I'll cope, Mum,' I tell her. 'When can you come home?'

'Don't be silly Guss, *I'll* cope,' says Daddy.

I feel proud of him. He's come to our rescue in our time of need. Mum looks lovingly at him. Maybe they will get back together. Perhaps I should put off Alistair? Daddy will look after both of us. I feel suddenly hopeful that everything will be all right in the end. Our family *will* have a happy ending. I tell Mum about the hoard of hidden treasure we found.

'I didn't know you'd kept anything,' she accused him. 'You said you wanted nothing to do with anyone dead.'

'You don't know everything.'

'Yes, well, you always were good at hiding things.'

'Daddy, you like old movies and they're full of dead people. Isn't Jeanne Moreau dead?'

'Gussie, shut up.'

'But she's your favourite actor.' I'm trying hard to defuse the scene. It seems they can't spend more than five minutes together without falling out. I should never have mentioned the camera. They were getting on fine before that.

'Mum, I couldn't find pyjamas or a nightie for you.'

'I don't have any, Gussie. I can't sleep if I'm wearing something. I get tangled up in the night.' She giggles. 'You'll never be able to stick me in an old people's home. The staff would be traumatised seeing me naked every morning.

'Jackson,' she says to Daddy, 'will you bring in my other glasses, please? My spare reading specs – the green ones, and I better have the red ones too if you can find them.'

'What movie do you want to watch, Guss?' Daddy is the best person in the world to watch a favourite movie with. We always speak the dialogue together. I don't fancy anything serious like Truffaut, and I don't really want to watch a Bollywood. Not *Fantasia* – boring. Not Busby Berkeley. Not *Kes*, too sad. Maybe an Indiana Jones movie, or *Waterworld?* Yes, *Waterworld*. I've only seen it three times. Hopefully it's not a prophetic story. The world is flooded and survivors have made islands from old tankers and docks. The baddies are thugs on jet skis and they are called Smokers. They kidnap a child who has the tattoo of a map of where to find dry land on her back. It's almost as exciting as an *Indiana Jones* movie but with interesting low-tech inventions, like a hot-air balloon made of animal skins and the hero's boat, which has a sail made from cloth and skins.

I go to bed early, thankful that Daddy is the next room. I have daydreams of him always being there with me, watching old movies and showing me how to make photographs. Perhaps he could be my manager or agent and get me loads of important projects for glossy magazines. He could be my mentor, my guide; maybe I could even make movies if he would show me how.

Daddy watches me take my drugs and writes down the times and amounts on Mum's chart. He takes me to the pet shop for mealworms and birdseed. I think he likes the birdfeeders in his garden, even though Alistair bought them. I feed Mr Robin some mealworms and get him to photograph me.

'Very impressive. I'll forget to feed the birds when you go home, you know that, don't you?'

'Of course you won't. You couldn't forget Mr Robin. He'll remind you with a song. Wouldn't you like a pet, Daddy? Don't you miss the cats?'

'No I don't. Damned hair everywhere. Can you imagine that all over my suede sofas?' He laughs and strokes my hair, attempting to flatten the spikes.

'You don't really prefer furniture to cats?'

'You talking to me?' he asks in a Robert de Niro voice, moving around like de Niro did to watch himself in the mirror. 'You talking to me?'

I smile. He does it so well.

'Yes, actually. Gussie, I know it's sad but I do prefer well-designed, comfortable and beautiful furniture to cats.' He smiles ruefully. Ruefully means that he wishes he didn't feel that but he does. Poor Daddy, what a sad life. You can't talk to sofas or cuddle them. He's happy now the man with a machine has cleaned the carpet.

No chance to learn a new word today. I'm very tired.

CHAPTER ELEVEN

I AM LOOKING into an open grave where my mother is wrapped in a bloody shroud. I'm falling...

'Shh, shh, it's okay, honeybun, you're having a bad dream.'

'Oh Daddy, Daddy...' I weep onto his shoulder. The towelling dressing gown, rough on my cheek, soaks up my tears.

MRS THOMAS! I had completely forgotten about her eye operation. I phone and she's at home. She's got her cat, Shandy to keep her company and she's feeling all right, but a bit sore. She's not surprised about Mum being in hospital, she says: 'I saw it coming.'

I phone Claire to see how my cats are. Gabriel answers.

'Your cats are silly. They're scared of ducks and rabbits. The cockerel hates them – chases them whenever he sees them. Charlie sits in my tree-house with me.'

'How are they getting on with the puppy?'

'Zennor? She's frightened of them. Puts her tail between her legs and runs and hides.'

'She doesn't? How sweet!'

'When are you coming home, Gussie?'

'I don't know, not as soon as I thought. Mum will have to recover from her operation first. I'll let you know. Is your mum there?'

'I'll get her. Gussie, I have a new pet.'

'Have you? What is it?'

'You won't tell Claire will you? It's a secret pet.'

'Tell me, Gabriel. What is it?'

'It's a spider.'

I imagine he means a house spider that he has put in a shoe-box or something. I'm reminded of a terrible thing I did once, when I was very little. I found a crab on the beach at Shoeburyness and wanted to keep it, but was told I couldn't. I smuggled it home with me and I hid it in a box under my bed. It died, of course. The smell was so bad, Mum found out. She gave me such a hard time. Poor crab.

'I like spiders,' I say.

'It's a humungous spider, Gussie, Billy gave it to me. I swapped him a grass snake.'

'I've never seen a grass snake.'

'I'll find you one when you come home. My spider's a red-kneed tarantula. I call him Terry the Terrible. He was called Ivan the Terrible but he looks more like a Terry.'

'A real tarantula? Wow! Is it a free-range spider?'

'What do you mean?'

'Does it hunt for its own food?'

'No, he's in a terrarium under my bed.'

'What does it eat, Gabriel?'

'Whatever I catch. I have to go now. Don't tell Claire about Terry. She doesn't like spiders. Claire! Claire, it's Gussie for you.'

I wonder what Claire will think next time she cleans under his bed. And what does a large spider eat? Large insects? Small birds? Mice? Must look it up.

'Gussie, hello darling, how are you? How's your mother? Is your father with you?'

'Yes, he is.'

'That's good. Let me know if you need me. I can come any time.'

She says it's all right for our cats to stay there for as long as they need to. That's one problem solved. My cats are fine, anyway. They're happy.

When we visit Mum, I take a bottle of elderflower cordial.

'No whisky?' she says.

'Sorry.'

'You could have disguised it in the elderflower bottle,' she says.

'Nah, don't think so.'

I lean over and she kisses me and strokes my cheek.

'Thank you for rescuing me,' she says. 'What would I do without you?'

I feel proud and sad, and my eyes smart. I tell her Claire sends her love.

'Yes, Jackson, you really should meet your relations – such nice people, surprisingly so in fact.'

'Mum!' I say, threateningly.

We open our mail, which has been sent on by Mrs Thomas, including my copy of *Bird Magazine*. Mum suggests I send them photos of me feeding Mr Robin mealworms from my hand. What a good idea. It might be the breakthrough I need to make me a famous wildlife photographer, except that Daddy would have taken the picture.

'Are you taking your medicines? Filling in the charts? How do you feel Gussie? My poor baby.' She cries on my arm and makes my sleeve wet. 'I'm sorry this happened, darling.' Her nose is red. Mum-Nose Pink – another colour chart name.

'I'm fine, really. When can you leave hospital, Mum?'

'Wednesday, if I'm good.'

But she isn't good. Wednesday comes and when Daddy goes to collect her she is in tears. Her temperature is up and she has an infection. She's in a room on her own and I am not allowed to go in to see her.

Alistair will not be here tomorrow. He's stuck in Bulgaria by an air controllers' strike. Bad luck always seems to come in threes. Sure enough – when I get back, on the patio step, there's Mr Robin – dead. He has been chewed and his breast is bloody. A cat attack, probably. I have seen a mangy, pregnant female skulking in the bushes.

I am the only mourner at Mr Robin's funeral. I bury him under the beech tree, after saying a few words: 'I only knew you a short time but I loved your voice and you brought happiness to me.' My sad words make me cry. I sing the first verse of *All Things Bright and Beautiful*. Sparrows and a blackbird hop around at the back of the garden keeping a respectful distance; rooks in the high branches are suitably dressed in black. I place a few sprigs of hebe and a daffodil on the grave and a cross made of two twigs tied with cotton. I know he wasn't Christian, but it makes me feel better. When I was little I used to make graves for butterflies, mice, shrews and lizards. Anything the cats half ate I would carefully place in a matchbox or wrap in tissue and bury in the garden. Now I leave the corpses for burying beetles to lay their eggs on and bury – Nature's recyclers.

Mr Robin was different. We had a special relationship. He trusted me. Into my mind has popped a book I had when I was small – *The Wise Robin* – a Ladybird Book. He too was called Mr Robin – Bob to his wife. She wanted tinsel from a Christmas tree to decorate her nest and persuaded her husband to get it. He was trapped on the tree inside the house on Christmas Day and a child, assuming he was a toy bird, wanted him as a present. He had to sing to prove he was real and then they let him out – minus the tinsel. When the tree was thrown out after Christmas there were pieces of tinsel still on it and so Mrs Robin had her smart shiny decor after all.

It's been too sad to learn a new word.

CHAPTER TWELVE

FORSAKE—TO DESERT; ABANDON

ANTHROPOLOGIST—SOMEONE WHO STUDIES THE SCIENCE OF
MAN IN ITS WIDEST SENSE (*sounds like it should be someone
who apologises for man*)

MUMMY STILL HAS an infection and is being kept in a separate
room, so still no visiting for me. Daddy goes in the afternoon
for half an hour and then is back.

'Gussie, I have to go somewhere. Will you be all right?'

No, I won't, is what I want to say but, 'Fine, no probs,'
comes out of my mouth. 'How long will you be?'

'Oh, a good couple of hours.'

'I'll come with you.'

'No, you can't do that, no. Take your pills if I'm not back.
Watch a movie. Phone Willy if you need anything. I've told
him I have to go out. Have a meeting with...'

'Why can't I come with you?' I don't listen to his reasons.
A man's gotta do what a man's gotta do.

It's raining too hard to go out for a walk. Didn't go
yesterday either. I walk around the flat for twenty minutes
instead. I pretend the sofa is the lake with swans and ducks
floating by; the side table is a block of shops, the vase of
orange dahlias is the flower seller's stall. I stop to pat a
spaniel puppy (a stool) and talk to a jogger (the coat rack)
who is doing up her laces. *What a lovely day. Do you come
here often? Only when it rains.*

I could phone the police and shop Daddy for leaving me
on my own, I'm sure it's illegal. I'm only twelve, for goodness

sake. I think you have to fourteen to be left on your own at home.

It could be worse: he could have asked the Snow Queen to look after me. I have a sulk, blowing bubbles with my spit as I did when I was little. I squeeze out a few tears, missing home, wishing Mum was here, wishing Mr Robin hadn't been killed, wishing I hadn't had a heart and lung transplant, wishing I was a million miles away and someone else.

Who would I like to be?

David Attenborough, I think. He spends all his time travelling to interesting natural places and learning all about insects and birds and animals. That sounds like a perfect job to me.

I start to watch some boring cartoons then give up after half an hour. Instead I make a recording of the rain. Maybe I could be a sound recordist for radio. That must be a really interesting job, listening to birds, animals, night sounds in forests, traffic sounds, sea sounds, the sounds a house makes when it is empty of people.

At home we have a catalogue from an exhibition of pictures made by the tracks that wild creatures make at dusk. The artist the animals' scratch marks and scatterings, worm slitherings and frog jump marks – on a glass plate coated on one side with a layer of carbon. A beetle's footprints look like tiny tank tracks. A slowworm made a pattern like someone cleaning windows, great smears and swirls of white on the blackened glass plate. There's one picture made up of the prints of a cat and a mouse. The cat's paw-prints look like a dinosaur's compared with the tiny mouse prints.

Carbon doesn't hurt the animals. It's the one element that all living things share in common. It forms the building blocks of life, and is 'the ultimate destiny of all life.' Perhaps I could do a sound version of that. The tiny scratching of ants marching; badgers snuffling and their long sharp claws digging for worms. That's their main food. They must have to work hard to get enough to fill them up. When we lived on the cliff we put out peanuts and leftovers for the badgers. They ate fish and chips, chicken carcasses, curry, anything except green vegetables. They were probably the best-fed badger family in Cornwall, if not the world. Now we're gone they'll have to make do with worms, bugs and slugs – their usual diet.

When I play back the recording I hear what sounds like Mr Robin's alarm call, a constant *wheep*, *wheep*, and I go to the patio door to look to see what he's making such a fuss about, before I remember that he is dead. There's a small bundle of sodden fluff on the step. I slide the door open. It's a kitten, about five or six weeks old. Poor little thing, it's shivering and half drowned. I pick him up and he spits and hisses at me, trying to look fierce but he's frightened. I wrap him in a towel and dry him carefully. It's a tom I think, you can't really tell at this age – completely black. Where's his mother? It's raining too hard for me to go out and search. Maybe his mother is the scruffy stray that killed Mr Robin? Why didn't she take the bird for her other babies to eat? Some mother! Or maybe she's old and sick and can't feed her babies properly and has had to leave each one on someone's doorstep, hoping they will be adopted.

I find a boot box and line it with one of my T-shirts. How am I going to feed him? I find an eyedropper in the bathroom cabinet and try feeding the kitten with warm milk mixed with raw egg. He doesn't like it, but licks his lips and wipes it off his chin with his paws in a very adult cat way. He is still shivering, from cold or fear. His paw pads are black and his eyes are the colour of forget-me-nots. What shall I call him? I give him a saucer of water mixed with a very little milk. His nose hits the water first and he draws back in surprise. He laps with difficulty, almost falling into it in his haste to drink. I find a tin of tuna and mash up a little. He likes that. Oh yes, he does like that.

He's now stretched out, fat belly up on my lap, purring loudly. He's so happy. I'll call him Happy, or maybe Sunny. Look at the time! Daddy said two hours but it's two and a half hours since he went out. He'll be home any time now. Oh God, what am I to do? I take the kitten to my room and put him in his box in the wardrobe, but Daddy still has clothes there. I'll put the box with the sleeping kitten under my bed for now and work out a plan later. I remember reading somewhere that kittens who have just left their mother are happier if they feel the pulse of a clock, like a heart beat, so I wrap up Mum's travel alarm clock in a flannel and place it by the kitten. It would drive me potty if I had to sleep with a clock. I think he might be cold, so I fill my hot water bottle for him and wrap one of Mum's woolly scarves around it so he doesn't burn himself. He looks very cosy. The rain's stopped, so I go out and look in the shed. It smells of cat. There's a nest of old newspapers in a corner, slightly bloody. This is where my kitten was born. No sign of the rest of the litter. The mother must have moved them. They do that all the time, if they think there's danger.

The phone rings.

'Gussie, it's me. How's Daddy managing? Is he looking after you?'

'Yes, Mum. Guess what I've found…'

'Get him for me, I need to talk to him.'

'He's not actually here at the moment…'

'Not there? Where the bloody hell is he? He's supposed to be taking care of you.'

'Don't panic, I'm fine. He had to go out. I'm cooking

supper tonight anyway – pasta and tuna.' (I hope the kitten has left enough tuna for the sauce.) 'Gussie, I'm so sorry this has happened.' She's crying.

'Don't be silly, you can't help it.' I'm crying too. In the end I don't tell her about the kitten. I'll save it for when she's feeling better. She's got enough worries.

Another phone call, very faint. Alistair still in Bulgaria, expecting a flight out tomorrow but will have to go straight back to work. He'll try and get to see Mum before he gets on the train to Cornwall. I think that's what he said.

Daddy takes me for my check-up and biopsy. He's attentive and solemn. 'You're a brave girl, Guss, I'm proud of you,' he says, and I feel warm inside. The nurses are all agog – what a silly word! They think he's handsome. Well, he is: as handsome as a film star. Maybe I should take this opportunity, when he's feeling positive about me, to tell him about the kitten? But he's flirting with Soo Yong, the pretty cardiac nurse; the moment passes. Anyway, I know he won't want to keep it, what with his cream furnishings and hectic life.

Precious is here today, also having tests. He doesn't look too happy.

When we are alone – Daddy has gone for a coffee – I tell him about the kitten. He isn't listening.

'What's up, Presh? Is something wrong?'

'Yes, Gussie. My father and sisters cannot get out of the country. There are too many problems.'

'I'm sorry.' He looks so sad and I feel useless. I put out my hand and touch his. It's cold and smooth. 'Would you like to visit us?'

'In London?'

'Yes. We're staying at my father's flat in Southend Green,

it's near the Heath. You could see my kitten.'

'I would like that.' His smile is huge. I remove my hand. I think of Brett, who took my hand to help me when we stepped out of a boat in the dark in the Scillies.

We swap telephone numbers and addresses. Everything is fine with my tests. No more rejection – touch wood. Mum is making me superstitious. She's always touching wood. I never used to but now I do. It can't hurt. I also throw spilt salt over my shoulder. In fact I use my left hand to throw it over my right shoulder, then my right hand to throw some over my left shoulder, just in case.

'Can we stop at the chemist's on the way home for a new hot water bottle?'

'What's wrong with the old one?'

'Perished.' I'm such a good liar. Must watch that.

There's a new robin in the garden. He isn't so brilliantly scarlet-breasted as the late Mr Robin, but he sings beautifully. I've put out crumbs for him, no mealworms. I better not tempt him to get too friendly in case the stray gets him. I would love to be able to tame the stray, but I haven't seen her since I found the kitten. Perhaps she's lying low, or she's gone travelling, on the hunt for another mate. I wonder what happened to her other kittens?

Daddy and I go to see Mum. She's in an ordinary ward now, sharing with three other women. One of them keeps sitting up and shouting, 'Jesus loves you!' An elderly man with red-rimmed eyes keeps wandering by wearing a backless hospital gown and wheeling his drip stand. I try not to look at his skinny bare bum. *One Flew Over the Cuckoo's Nest*, or what? Mum looks worse than she did before, I think, though Daddy doesn't seem to notice. Alistair has visited and got the train back to Cornwall.

'I can't stay much longer with Gussie, Lara. I have to go away in a week's time.'

'But I thought you said…'

'Something's come up.'

'Oh, God, Jackson, can't you ever think of anyone except yourself?' People are staring at us. I leave them to it. I'm no good at trying to keep the peace. The old lady sits up and points at me: 'Jesus loves you!'

I have made the kitten a litter tray from a stainless steel baking dish lined with paper and earth. I haven't seen Daddy do much cooking in his glossy kitchen apart from opening tins and microwaving things so I don't think he'll miss it. I keep my door closed with a notice blue-tacked on – PRIVATE, NO ENTRY – if he wants to come in for something, I just hope the kitten is out of the way. Mother cats don't recognise their kittens after they've been missing for a couple of days, so there's no point in trying to find her and reintroduce Sunny into the litter.

Sunny is less frightened of me now, though he still hisses when I go to pick him up. He looks so funny, fur on end, black whiskers twitching, cornflower eyes glaring at me. His little claws are very sharp. He is so black when his eyes are closed I can't tell which end is which, even with my specs on. When I put him in the tray, after each meal, he tries to eat the earth, licking at it, or tumbles over on his nose, his little tail stuck up straight like a quivering coiled wire.

When Daddy goes out I take the kitten on a tour of the flat. We sit on the sofa and watch *Bambi* but I start crying even before the bit where Bambi's mother dies, so I turn off. I feed him some tinned sardines and he eats far too much and is sozzled, round-tummied and completely out of it. What am I going to do with him? I'm sure Daddy would love him if he gave him a chance. Perhaps not, though.

The phone rings.

'Gussie, it's Claire. I'm coming up tomorrow to look after you.'

'Oh, Claire, are you really? That's wonderful. Does Mum know?'

'Yes, I've spoken to her. Don't do anything. I'll look after myself. Sleep on the floor, if I have to. I'm catching the twelve noon from St Erth, so I'll be with you about five. I'll get a taxi from Paddington.'

As I replace the phone I discover that my cheeks are wet.

Mum phones: 'Gussie, has Claire phoned? Good. I feel happier knowing she'll be with you. I haven't told your father, will you tell him, please?'

When Daddy returns I tell him about Claire. I think he's relieved. After all, he has a full time job and can't keep taking time off to look after me.

'So, you'll meet one of your relations soon. She's not actually one of our blood relations; she's only connected by marriage. Anyway, I know you'll like her.'

'*M'chutin*,' he says.

'Bless you.'

'No, *M'chutin*. It's a Hebrew word that means related by marriage.'

'Oh.' I didn't realise Daddy was so knowledgeable about anything other than film.

'How do you know Hebrew?'

'Can't remember. Willy? Jewish girl I used to know? Woody Allen movie? Can't remember.' He sniffs. 'What's that horrible fishy smell, Gussie?'

'Tinned fish – I can't get enough of it. It's really good for me.'

Daddy sits on the sofa and gets bitten by a cat flea.

'Where the hell did that come from?'

'You must have picked it up at your girlfriend's,' I say spitefully. I make a mental note to buy a flea comb when we next go to the pet shop or I could get a nit comb from the chemist in the village.

'Hope this Claire is good at housework,' he grumbles, hoovering his suede upholstery. 'It's like the *Invasion of the Body Snatchers* in here.'

Willy and I walk to the Heath next morning. He is a quiet companion, a good listener. I tell him about the kitten.

'What are you going to do with the *kleine Katze*? You can't hide him forever.'

'Yes, I can, I'll take him back to Cornwall.'

'But will your other cats tolerate a kitten?'

'Rambo won't mind. I don't know about Charlie and Flo. They might be jealous.'

'Yes, and they will be resentful of your attention to this kitty and maybe they will bully him.'

I hadn't thought of that. All I had thought of was rescuing a poor lost kitten, but Willy's right. Charlie especially will be very angry with me for forsaking her and having a new pet. I haven't told Mum about him yet either.

At the bridge over the railway line Willy opens a gate.

'Would you like to see my vegetable garden?'

'Where? Here?'

'Yes, my allotment. *Kommen sie hier*.' I follow him along the path to a series of little plots alongside the railway line. In each one there is someone digging.

'*Guten morgen*, Willy,' shouts an old lady in red wellies and a long mac. I think she is German too.

'*Guten morgen*, Anna.'

He greets and is greeted by the gardeners, who are mostly old and foreign. A man in a green bobble hat waves to us and says something in Italian. Willy introduces me to him. 'This is my good friend, Julio. He grows the best potatoes and broad beans in Hampstead.'

'No, no, I grow the best everything!' Julio shouts. 'Marrow, aubergine, fennel, carrot, tomato, oregano.' Then he starts singing – something from an opera it sounds like.

Willy's allotment has a little old apple tree on a rectangular vegetable plot, and a wooden shed with a real horseshoe on the door.

'I make you a cup of tea, ya?'

'Yes please.' I don't really like tea but any hot drink would be good, just to keep my hands warm.

Oh, the smell of it! Earth and onions. Willy's shed is full of hooks with spades and forks and other tools hanging on them. There's a string of onions and sunflowers drying upside down. He has a shelf of books in German, a pair of wellington boots, a dented kettle, a primus stove and two chipped enamel mugs. A solid lump of sugar sits in a torn paper bag. There are old shopping baskets under a table with bruised apples in them. It smells warm and leafy, like a greenhouse. It reminds me of my Grandma's garden shed. Actually, it was Grandpop's shed, not Grandma's. He used to mend their shoes in there on a metal thingy that looked like three feet. I went in once looking for him and walked into two dead chickens hanging by their feet from the ceiling, dark musty feathers, black blood dripping onto the floor.

We sit on two wooden boxes against the sunny wall of the shed and dip wholemeal biscuits into hot sweet tea. Willy pours whisky from a hip flask into his. A thrush dips his beak into the dark earth and pulls on the tail of a long worm. The bird tugs and tugs and still the worm hangs on, but the worm loses the tug-of-war and the thrush beats it onto a stone, and when it becomes mushy and presumably dead, he swallows it.

Every creature hangs onto life. Even the kitten's fleas, when I have maimed them between my finger nails, try desperately to hop or crawl away. They cling to life just as much as an elephant or a whale. Just as much as I do.

It is so peaceful here, even with trains going by. Commuters stare out of the dirty windows at us.

Willy takes off his coat and shoes and changes into his wellies. He rolls up his shirtsleeves and I see he has blue numbers tattooed above his wrist. My stomach drops suddenly and I see in my mind a picture of Auschwitz dead, piled together like the white bones of birds. The Italian man is still singing and the lady in red wellies is weeding with a long-handled hoe. I feel suddenly faint, so I sit down while Willy digs happily in his small patch of London clay.

'Thank you for the tea and biscuits, Herr Weinberger. I do like your garden.'

'Here, Gussie, you must take some apples. They are last year's crop and very sweet.'

I can't say no, even though I don't really want to carry a heavy bag. He must have seen the reluctance in my face.

'*Ach, nein*, I forget your operation. I will deliver them to you later, yes?'

Phew. That was a lucky escape.

I do like old people. Walking back, I think again of Grandma in their Essex garden. She grew most of the things she and Grandpop ate – potatoes, carrots, onions, runner beans (though Grandpop built the bamboo pole wigwams they climbed up) lettuces, radishes, raspberries, strawberries, blackcurrants, gooseberries and loganberries.

When I was told that Grandpop and Grandma had

died I felt as if someone had struck me with a knife in my heart, and that sharp pain came back each time I woke and remembered, for a long time. But now the pain is familiar; I don't think of it every morning. I have found a corner for it where I can take it out and look at it and then put it back again, like an old photograph or a movie that makes me cry even though I know what happens.

The French onion man is wheeling his bike along the road. I hope he doesn't try to ride it, he looks like he's spent the last three hours in the pub.

I go to the newsagent for some chocolate. (I am allowed chocolate, though I have to watch my cholesterol and sodium levels.)

There are two women with buggies in the shop and the babies are gurgling at each other, as if they are having a very interesting conversation. I've noticed that babies are always fascinated by each other; toddlers always look at toddlers and teenagers are mostly interested in teenagers. It's as if humans prefer to tune in to others at their own stage of development. Maybe I could study anthropology at uni?

I can't wait to go to school and meet other twelve-year-olds.

I'm a freak, always hanging out with adults and old people. It's not normal. It's not fair.

CHAPTER THIRTEEN

NO TIME FOR new words today – too hectic.

The Snow Queen comes with Daddy to the flat to meet me. I have luckily just fed the kitten, he's had a poo and now he's asleep under my bed, hopefully, but I haven't had a chance to clean his litter tray.

Annika is not the bimbo I expected. She's a part-time model, yes, but also she's training to be a lawyer and she's from Sweden. She bosses Daddy terribly, making him get her a decaffeinated coffee and look for pearls she thinks she has left here. She opens the bedroom door and turns up her small nose in horror. I push in front of her.

'Excuse me, *I'll* look in *my* bedroom.'

The doorbell rings. The Snow Queen goes to open it, and closes it again.

She shouts something in Swedish to Daddy. Daddy opens the door and laughs.

'That's not a tramp, that's Willy in his gardening gear,' he says, kissing her. Willy has the apples.

Willy smiles scornfully at the Snow Queen and winks at me. I'd like to kill her. Perhaps I'll start reading thrillers to get some ideas on how to perform the perfect murder.

I find the pearls under the bed and practically throw them at her. The Snow Queen has a sneezing fit and discovers a flea bite on her ankles. Is furious. Glares at me as if I am flea-ridden. Says Daddy should get a pest controller to clean the entire flat, and when he has he can call her. Slams the door on her way out. Well done, kitten.

'Gussie, tell me the truth. Have you brought a cat into my flat?'

'Daddy, where would I get a cat?' Oh dear, what's the matter with me? I should have confessed.

'When's this woman Claire arriving?'

'Tea-time, I think. She's going to find her own way here, don't worry. And she's not This Woman, she's your relation.' Oh dear, I sound like Mum.

Daddy makes up the sofa-bed with clean linen and puts his old sheets in the washing machine.

'I didn't know you could speak Swedish, Daddy.'

'Oh, yes, comes from my Bergman era.'

He has to go to his office in the afternoon so I go to see Mum on my own.

'Are you keeping your daily log, darling?'

'Yes, Mum.'

'How do you feel?'

'Okay. Nausea, a bit.' I don't tell her I'm feeling practically suicidal. I know it's one of the drugs and I just have to get on with it.

'I had to keep a daily log when you were a baby.'

'Did you?'

'Yes, I had to give you Digoxin every four hours, night and day. If I didn't write it down straight away after giving it to you, I wouldn't know if I *had* given it. I was so exhausted I was hallucinating.'

'Poor Mum.'

'I don't know how you survived. I was a hopeless mother.'

'Well, I did, so you must have done something right.'

'Yes, and look at you! I'm so proud of you.'

Horror of horrors! – When I was out the kitten escaped from the bedroom and scratched the back of the sofa-bed. He also vomited on the duvet and it dribbled onto the suede. I think I gave him too much pilchard in tomato sauce this morning.

I don't have the foggiest notion how to remove the stain. It's really bad. It looks like murder has been committed. *St Valentine's Day Massacre*. I try with washing liquid but the stain spreads. I scrub it with a nailbrush but that just makes it wetter.

When Daddy gets back, I say it was me who was sick. He doesn't notice the scratches, luckily, as the vomit stain is so gross. He is very good about it. I suggest we cover it with a cushion but he says we'll still smell it. He phones a caretaker or someone, to come and take the sofa-bed away, and orders another one which will take twelve weeks to be made and delivered, and only then thinks to ask me if I am all right now and suggests we go to the hospital – my hospital, not Mum's. He assumes I have been vomiting blood. But I convince him I'm fine, say I had too many pilchards in tomato sauce.

'Where will Claire sleep?' I ask.

'The surviving sofa.' He gets out yet another set of bed linen, and has to go out to buy another duvet as the other one was 'beyond salvation'. Mum would buy a second-hand sofa if we were at home, but Daddy only likes new things, apart from movies. He's got to buy new towels too.

Now I'm in a flat with no bed for my mother when she comes out of hospital, my father is mostly absent and I'm looking after a destructive fleabag. Sunny has taken to climbing the blinds in the bedroom. They are white pleated fabric and he runs up the side of them and sits on the top. He is now called Fleabag or Bad Boy. He purrs at both names and climbs my legs. Luckily he doesn't scratch through my combat trousers. Funny little thing, he still hisses and spits when I pick him up. He is so black – black paw pads, black nose, black whiskers, midnight coat, the darkest winter's night on the Cornish moors with not even a sliver of moon; he is the total lack of light, the deepest lake, the darkest forest, the angel of darkness, Beelzebub. He is Beelzebub. Not sure how to pronounce that – is it Beel or Be-el? Anyway, it suits him. Beelzebub. You bad, bad cat. I like it. He likes it. It's an important name. I think it might mean the Prince of Darkness, or the Devil.

Claire hugs me gently. 'You look wonderful, Gussie, what a change! You look so well, I can't believe it.' It's funny how if someone tells you you look awful, you immediately feel bad, and if they tell you you look *good,* well, you suddenly feel good. It must be psychological.

'It's lovely to meet you, Claire,' says Daddy. 'Will you go and see Lara this evening or are you too tired from the journey?'

'No, I'm not in the least bit tired. Oh thanks, that's plenty.' Daddy has poured wine for them both.

'I have a bit of catching up to do, so if you take Gussie…'

'Of course. Is that all right? Can you walk that far, Gussie?'

'Yes, it's only a couple of hundred yards down the road. I'm fine.'

Claire has brought me presents: a jigsaw from my little cousin Gabriel, that he made himself. He's painted a picture of his puppy, Zennor, pasted it onto thin wood and then sliced it up into little pieces with a special tool in his father's workshop.

'It's lovely. He's very clever.'

'Yes, he's a chip off the old block.' We laugh.

She's brought Cornish clotted cream and fudge – much better than the supermarket ones. Best of all, there are photographs of my cats – Charlie in Gabriel's tree house, Flo looking cross at a chicken; Rambo cringing from a rabbit.

I offer Claire another glass of wine but she says she'd rather have a cup of tea and she's brought her own herbal teabags.

'Show me the kitchen, I'll do it.'

After lots of news of my cats and my cousins, she suddenly remembers another present from my great-aunt Fay: it's a hand-made, bright pink and orange felt bag, with a shoulder strap. Very girlie. I can't imagine ever wearing it. I'd have preferred a camouflage or khaki Army surplus rucksack. But it was a kind thought. Maybe I'll hang it in my room with socks in.

Claire holds my arm and we walk slowly through the dark, down the road to the village, past the gate to the allotments and the railway line, across the road and past the pharmacy and the shops still open, then up Pond Street to the hospital.

I haven't seen Mum smile so much since Alistair was here. They gossip and I talk to the person in the next bed, who hasn't got any visitors. She's had a similar operation to Mum except that hers wasn't an emergency. Her three children and husband are at a school concert tonight.

School concerts! I wonder if St Ives School has concerts? I don't even know if I can act. I can't play any instrument. Or at least, I've never tried. I suppose if Mum or Daddy had been musical they would have encouraged me, bought a piano or a violin, but they aren't and they didn't. Perhaps Phaedra would let me try her drum kit? The Jesus Loves You woman has left or died and the bare-bottomed old man is nowhere to be seen, thank goodness. I wish I was a boy. I don't think males have as much trouble with their insides as females do.

For supper Daddy makes us cheese omelette with a green salad and we sit around the table together. At home we'd sit on the floor at the low table and watch telly while we ate.

'So, I hear Gussie and Lara knew you before Gussie discovered that you were related to me?'

'That's right. She's a clever girl, researching and all that sort of thing. Moss's mother Fay is your late father's sister. It's a shame you lost touch with your family.'

'Yes, well, Gussie's trying to reform me. Make me more family-conscious.'

'Nothing wrong with that. Nothing wrong with families. Anyway, I'll stay as long as I'm needed,' Claire says, tucking into her dinner.

'I'll be off then,' says Daddy. He has a black leather holdall on his shoulder.

'I'm sorry I'm turning you out of your own home. I didn't think,' says Claire.

'No it's fine, that's okay. No problemo. I can sleep at the office.'

'I thought you were staying with Boadicea?' I say.

'Annika! Yes, well, when she's calmed down, maybe.'

'She's a bit Bette Davis,' I say to him, picking out the anchovies and putting them on the side of my plate. I wonder if Beelzebub would like them?

'Yeah, well, she is a bit.' He smiles smugly as if being a drama queen is a good thing.

'Sorry there's no proper bed, Claire, but we've had a few accidents lately. The sofa's pretty comfortable.'

'Why don't you phone Boadicea?'

'Annika.'

'Annika, and see if she's forgiven you?'

'Too soon. She might be Scandinavian, but she has a Mediterranean temperament. I'll give her a day or two.' He kisses me goodnight, and gives Claire a peck on the cheek.

So, maybe his girlfriend is not the *Snow Queen* – more of

a *Tank Girl* or *Red Sonia*? Terrifying, anyway.

Daddy safely out of the way and the dishes stacked in the dishwasher, I fetch the kitten. I tell Claire how I found him and that Daddy doesn't know anything about him, and mustn't be told.

'What a sweet kitty. Why mustn't he know?'

'He's given up cats and children. He says he prefers furniture.'

Beelzebub is nocturnal, as most cats are, and races about chasing his toys and invisible mice and having fun until he suddenly falls asleep inside the felt bag.

'Thanks for coming to rescue us, Claire.' I kiss her goodnight.

'My pleasure. It's lovely to see you looking so well. We've all been worried about you.'

Mum comes home today. I've cooked a chocolate cake. She's always showing me how to cook things, and now it's come in useful. Daddy fetches her, while I kill fleas. They are difficult to see on Beelzebub's black fur, but he has loads. Luckily they are mostly of the pale brown variety. I enjoy the satisfying pop when I squash one between thumb and fingernails – difficult, though, as I have bitten my fingernails to the quick. Why is it called the quick?

What am I to do about Beelzebub? He is getting naughtier and naughtier – leaping from the curtain rail onto the bed and attacking me is his latest trick. I have made several small toys from string and twisted paper, which he enjoys chasing and killing. He climbs onto the bed when I am in it and sleeps curled up on my pillow. At least he hasn't torn the muslin curtains – yet. His tiny turds are easy to dispose of. I pluck them from the dirt with Mum's tweezers and put them down the lavatory.

Claire is making chicken pie.

'Mum!' We hug carefully.

'Claire, thank you so much. You're a star, you know that, don't you?'

Mum looks frail still and moves slowly, slower than me! She is going very grey. Daddy doesn't hang around.

'But aren't you staying for supper. Chicken pie?'

'Smells wonderful, but I have a date, sorry. Got everything you need? Then I'll be off. *Ciao* ladies.'

He kisses me and waves airily at Claire and Mum. He never was good with ill people. We girls eat an early supper – the yummy pie followed by my chocolate cake and we cuddle up on the remaining sofa.

'What's that?' Mum pinches something on her ankle. 'Oh my God, it's a cat flea. Gussie?'

'Yes, Mum, I know.'

'But how? We didn't import them from Cornwall, did we?'

'No, it's a NW3 cat flea.'

'Explain!'

I fetch Beelzebub, who for once is sleepy and gentle with me.

'Oh Gussie, where did it come from? Does your father know?'

I explain how the robin metamorphosed into a black cat.

'Oh, yeah, of course it did. You can't keep it, you know that, don't you?'

'Oh but why not?' I whine pitifully, hoping her maternal instincts will kick in to protect me from hurt and sorrow. No such luck.

'It's out of the question. Your father won't tolerate it. It's black, for goodness sake! Cream suede upholstery? You'll have to find it a new home.'

'It goes beautifully with his décor. Classic – black and white. Like photographs and old movies. He *ought* to have a black cat.' I admit to her that it was the kitten that ruined the sofabed and she hoots with laughter.

Mum has the kitten on her lap where it turns its full moon eyes on her. 'Oh, you're so beautiful! The kitten touches his nose to Mum's and turns round, tail up, so his bottom is facing her.

'Do you know why they do that?'

'No, why do they do that?'

'They expect you to sniff their bottoms, ' I tell her.

'Well, I think I'll forgo that pleasure,' she says, 'fragrant though it is, I'm sure. Is there any chicken left, Claire? I'm sure kitty would like some.'

We giggle together. It's so lovely to have Mum back. She examines the kitten's ears to see if he has mites, and is delighted to see I have managed to keep fleas to a minimum by daily grooming but says we will have to get some flea powder for the flat at the earliest opportunity. She says I'm not allowed to clean the litter tray any more in case of infection – cats carry a disease called toxoplasmosis, so she will do it until Beelzebub learns to go outside. A visit to the vet is planned, to make sure he is healthy and for anti-flea and anti-flu injections etc. I can't remember how old Charlie was when she had her anti-flu injections.

Mummy and I are sharing my bed: luckily it's king size. The kitten joins us, trying to catch our toes from the outside of the duvet, then curling up by Mum's head.

'He likes you.'

'She, he's a she,' Mum says.

'Oh, really? Well, she's called Beelzebub.'

'Good name,' says Mum. 'It's pronounced Be-elzebub. Seen my clock?'

'What clock?'

'Alarm clock, folds up, you know, red leather case.'

'Er...'

'I know I brought it with me. I seem to have mislaid my cream cashmere scarf too.'

'Night, Mum. It's so lovely to have you home.'

'Lovely to be out of that hard bed. God I hate hospitals. I didn't sleep a wink all the time I was there. And my own lavatory – bliss! Having to share with strangers is awful. And there Wasn't a Bidet.'

CHAPTER FOURTEEN

DECEASED — DEAD; LATELY DEAD

ONOMATOPOEIA — THE FORMATION OF A WORD IN IMITATION OF THE
SOUND OF THE THING MEANT; A WORD SO FORMED; THE USE OF WORDS
WHOSE SOUNDS HELP TO SUGGEST THE MEANING

CLAIRE IS GREAT, she's so organised. Makes our beds, opens
and closes stiff windows, does the washing and ironing and
hoovering. Mops the kitchen floor. Cleans the two lavatories,
the bath, shower and washbasins, the bidet; cleans the
kitchen sink, tidies the flat 'til it looks nearly as immaculate as
it did when we arrived, apart from all our clothes and books
and girlie stuff: knickers and their tights and bras hanging
up in the bathroom and shower room. She shops for food
and everything and does it all without any fuss. She's very
good at looking after people. It must be her physiotherapy
training and the fact that she has three children.

'How's Gabriel? Won't he be missing you?'

'He's okay. Back at school and busy with animals and his
tree house. It's Phaedra I'm worried about. She doesn't know
what she wants to do. She says she's going to study "Stuff".
Get a degree in "Stuff".'

'I thought she wanted to be a dancer.'

'Sure she does, but my god, every child in St Ives is all
singing and dancing. It seems the youth theatre has a lot to
answer for. The market will be flooded.'

'How's her drumming?'

'Don't know, she's banished to the shed at the other end
of the garden.' Claire is making chicken soup and apple
crumble, using Willy's apples.

Mum is oblivious to most things apart from her bowels. She's obsessed. Has to have pears in the morning or her bowels don't work. 'Haven't worked since the hysterectomy.' Her physio at the hospital told her to eat three pears a day, and she doesn't really like pears.

Linda, one of her London friends, comes round with a bag full of natural remedies, like arnica and vitamins and food supplements of zinc and silenium for Mum and a magazine for me, and while Claire takes time off to go shopping in Hampstead they spend the afternoon discussing their insides. They are laughing over a cartoon in the *Oldie* magazine: two middle-aged women drinking. '*Do you remember the days we used to sit around talking about what arseholes our husbands were? Now we just talk about our arseholes.*' I can't see what's funny about that.

The teen magazine is shocking, all about boys and snogging. I tried reading the stories that are supposed to be true ones, but they seem totally alien to my own life. Normal lives with normal problems like friendships that go wrong, girls with bitchy friends, girls who have period pains or pimples or girls who want to be pop stars. One story about a Russian girl whose brother made her pregnant. Ohmygod! Mum would not approve. I feel like hiding the magazine under the bed so she can't find it.

We are a couple of old crocks, sitting together in the evening after supper, comparing our aches and pains. The bathroom cabinet is our pharmacy, full of our combined medicines. Claire is very understanding and nods at Mum's complaining, and gently massages her back.

'Allowed alcohol, are you?' she asks as Mum pours herself a large whisky.

'Better the painkiller I know than the drugs I don't,' she replies. 'I recommend it. One for you?'

Using a pencil I rescue a fruit fly from Mum's whisky and examine in through Dad's Lupe (a magnifier especially for examining transparencies). Actually I thought it was dead and deceased, a late fruitfly, passed on, gone to the other side, fallen off its perch, pushing up daisies, but it sits on the pencil point, wiping its face with its forelegs, staggers around a bit and falls over. Now it's drying its face again and exploring the pencil. Whisky has damaged its brain. (It's damaged Mum's, Daddy reckons.) Mum always eats a fry-up when she has a hangover: eggs, bacon, fried bread, tomatoes and mushrooms; the full English. Then she needs sugar – chocolate, or fudge and lots of it. It works a treat, apparently. But she's always a bit wan that evening. Wan is a lovely word – onomatopoeic – woozy, weepy, weak, wilting – wan. Several minutes after I have removed the fruit fly from the whisky it seems to recover from the near drowning and soon it's flown. It will be back in Mum's single malt, betya. Yes, it's back, circling the glass for a hair of the dog that bit him. She ought to have one of those little cotton circular thingies with beads at the edge to put on top of her glass, like they used to have for milk jugs. Grandma had them. When I was little I used to wear them on my head, pretending to be a princess. I've seen them at car boot sales and thought how pretty they are. It's something I can look out for – a useful present. Oh dear, she's just spat it out. Mum, the fly. Poor fruitfly. I expect it died happy. That's better than being squashed *before* you've had a chance to taste a special single malt whisky.

It's Mum's birthday soon. April 1st. I don't know if we'll be back in St Ives for it, or will we be able to celebrate it with Daddy? I probably won't be able to find a doily or whatever it is called before then, unless I find one at the Hampstead antique market. We've been to no car boot sales here. I bet a Hampstead car boot would be brilliant. All the rich people could sell their old designer clothes and trainers and practically new furniture and antiques they are bored with. We could find all sorts of treasures, not like in Cornwall, where lots of the stall-holders are poor and are trying to sell clapped-out kids' clothes and toys.

I better remind Daddy about her birthday. It must be strange for him, for both of them, to be thrust together like this, when they've been apart for so long. Like being on a desert island with someone you hate but have to get along with in order to survive. My idea of hell is to be on a desert island with Siobhan – my rival in affection for Brett. She is girlie pretty, has a padded bra and a belly button ring and I hate her. Her little sister Bridget is cool. But Siobhan is definitely the woman in the *Three Musketeers*, Milady: no morals whatsoever, completely cold-blooded, played by Faye Dunaway. Called in the movie Lady de Winter. How funny – like the first Mrs de Winter in *Rebecca*. I've never known a de Anybody. I call Siobhan sss – which stands for… but my Grandma used to say – if you can't say something nice about someone, say nothing. So… I'll say nothing.

Moss phones and says that Gabriel is missing Claire badly and is living almost entirely in the tree, like Cosimo in Italo Calvino's *The Baron in the Trees*, who at the age of twelve, vowed to always live in trees. There's a problem with a pet spider that's gone AWOL, though Claire says she can't imagine what he means, as Gabriel hasn't got a pet spider, and Phaedra is staying out all night long doing goodness knows what on the back of a boy's motorbike, and he can't go searching for her as he has to stay and look after Gabriel, and Troy is being a pain in the arse, as ever. 'What's new?' says Claire.

Long discussions. Mum phones Daddy and they've come to a new arrangement. Claire is going home.

'I don't know what I would have done without you. Thanks Claire.' Mum cries as she says goodbye.

Claire says to me, 'You're a good girl, Gussie. Home soon, yeah?'

'Yes,' I say, 'we'll be home soon.'

Daddy comes each morning and is being very attentive. He does the washing and dusting and sorts the laundry but draws the line at ironing my pyjamas. I don't allow him in the bedroom as I can't hide the kitten anywhere else really. Mum isn't able to do much around the flat, and rests in the afternoon on the sofa. I can't do much either, like hoovering, which is a nuisance because there are still fleas. Also, *I* have to rest in the afternoon too.

I'm ploughing my way through *Gone with the Wind*. It's huge, heavy to hold in bed. Having seen the movie once (one of Mum's favourites) it's easy to follow and I keep imagining thingy with the thin moustache as Rhett Butler and Vivienne Leigh as Scarlett O'Hara. What a wonderful name! Why can't I be called something exciting like that? Augusta Stevens – I ask you, what sort of a name is that?

I do love reading better than anything. It's like dreaming – an escape into another world. I can become anyone and be part of another universe, forget my own problems and reality. When I finish a book, I'm lost until I can find another to immerse myself in. I suppose because of being ill and having to stay in bed lots and not go to school very often, I enjoy the other worlds I find in the pages. A book is a magic carpet that takes me anywhere, anywhen, anyhow. I can be waiting in my hospital bed for some horrible treatment, yet I'm a million miles away in another skin, the skin of a girl with a real working heart, who has a mother and father and brothers and sisters. I can be an ace pilot; a boy who lives with animals in the jungle; a brilliant detective; an American beauty a hundred years ago; I can be anyone. If I could be anyone in any book, who would I choose? That's difficult. Perhaps one of the family in *Swallows and Amazons*. Or George in the *Famous Five*, or Ellie, the girl narrator in the John Marsden book *Tomorrow when the War Began*; or Scarlett O'Hara. I love it when she tears down the green velvet curtains to make a dress.

Probably, actors escape into the character of the part they are playing, become them for a while.

Willy, dressed very smartly in a dark grey, double-breasted suit and with a blue tie has brought a huge bouquet of spring flowers; narcissus, daffodils and tulips, for both of his '*Schönen Frauen*'. They smell of Cornwall. The kitten jumps onto his lap.

'She likes you,' I say, but Willy is worried about his suit and the kitten soon jumps down.

Mum is searching the bathroom cabinet. 'Where did I put my tweezers?'

CHAPTER FIFTEEN

PROCEDURE—A MODE OF PROCESSING; A METHOD OF CONDUCTING
BUSINESS; A COURSE OF ACTION

SOME PEOPLE THINK that when you die your spirit or soul becomes another creature. If you have lived a good life you might become a more developed creature and if you've not been good you live again as a lower being – an ant or a beetle.

But who's to say what is higher or lower? How is a tiger, say, a higher creature than a hedgehog or a penguin? What's wrong with life as an inchworm? Okay, you might not have long to live, but you get to spend all your time outside eating marigolds or whatever.

Sounds pretty good to me. No pain, no anxiety, no worries about your parents not getting on or taking your pills at the right time. You simply eat and excrete – I suppose they do that, every creature does.

I would preferably like to come back as a cat – one of ours. They have such a fine life and if I had fur like my kitten or Charlie everyone would love me. Is it fur or hair? Perhaps if I am good enough in this life I will come back as a cat.

Not one in China, though. I saw a horrible programme on the news about how the Chinese treat some dogs and cats. They trap them, skin them alive and use their fur for clothes or even toys. Tigers are hunted or even farmed to be killed, and every part of the animal – not just the skin, but blood, bones, private parts, is sold for lots of money to be used in medicine by people who mistakenly think they are being made strong or virile. It's all too horrible to think about – poor innocent creatures cruelly killed for money.

I think I'll give up eating Chinese takeaways as a protest. I must remember to tell Mum to do the same.

Though, I suppose if you are an English Chinese restaurateur, you won't have the same culture as a Chinese person living in China, and you are not in the habit of killing dogs and cats. So I shouldn't punish them for the sins of the Chinese Chinese.

Phew! That means I can go on eating take away. Except for king prawn and other shellfish, of course.

I'm very lucky that most of the people I know are humane to each other and animals. Thinking about reincarnation: some people do believe in it – Hindus, I think. If a person has done bad things in one existence he returns after death as a lesser creature – a warthog or a wallaby, maybe. But how does a wallaby lead a good life in order to be reincarnated as a higher being? And is there a progression of higher and lower creatures? Who can tell if a cockroach is more worthy than a chicken? I read somewhere that cockroaches can live a week without a head. I think chickens can run around without a head too, but only for a few seconds. And what difference does the life of a chicken make to the world? At least while we are human we have the opportunity to make a difference, do something meaningful, even if it's only to have a child who will grow up to be someone who will make a difference, like Nelson Mandela or Mozart or Charles Darwin. Of course, one might have a child who becomes the next Adolf Hitler or Robert Mugabe, so each of us has to make the effort to do something worthwhile in our one life, like help orphans or make a beautiful piece of work, a painting or a poem or a novel that lasts forever.

Poem about reincarnation to send to Brett:

I wannabe
A wallaby.
Will you be
One too?

It's great not to have to hide the kitten from Mum, though she has suggested we keep her secret from Daddy for now. Beelzebub seems to have been the cause of rather a lot of destruction. Mum still hasn't decided what to do about her, whereas Beelzebub knows exactly what she wants – a warm soft bed, lots of strokes and petting, grooming each day, and plenty of Greek yoghurt and pilchards in tomato sauce. Daddy cancelled the hire car when Mum was in hospital but Claire found a corner shop that delivers. The driver is a young square-jawed Armenian, dishy, according to Mum, and he carries the groceries into the kitchen for her. We unpack together. I notice she has ordered plenty of kitten food so she can't be thinking of disposing of Beelzebub just yet.

'When are we going home, Mum?'

'We have to wait for your last biopsy and my six week check-up, but I see no reason why I can't travel on the train soon,' she says. 'Except that I can't carry luggage, and you certainly can't. I think the car might be more comfortable, if Alistair can take time off to collect us.'

'Couldn't Daddy take us back in his car?'

I have fantasies of Daddy arriving at our house and staying overnight and then falling in love with Mum all over again and staying forever. He could get a job as a film studies teacher at Falmouth University Art College.

'It might be fast, Gussie, but comfortable in the back seat? I don't think so. It's basically a two-seater, and then there's our luggage.'

And Beelzebub, I think.

'Anyway, he's got to go away again soon.'

'When? Who's going to drive me to hospital?'

'We'll get a bus or a cab, don't worry.'

My biopsies are uncomfortable procedures. They insert a catheter into a vein in my neck to go down into my heart and into the right ventricular myocardium. They do an x-ray so they can see the area where they are slicing off a piece of heart tissue. Afterwards, when the local anaesthetic wears off, I feel sore.

I hope we do get a cab.

A postcard from Mrs Thomas, with a picture of the harbour:

Dear Gussie,
Sad news. Shandy has passed away. He was 15 years old – a good age for a cat, but I miss him terribly. He has been my constant companion since my late husband passed away. My eye is settling down nicely. Give my best wishes to your mother and I hope you are both recovering from your operations as I am from mine.
Love to you both,
Mrs Thomas.

Our bodies are so fragile. We aren't well designed, us humans. Our skin breaks and bones crack and split and things go wrong so easily. Our cells don't do what they are supposed to do and become diseased. We are attacked by viruses.

Mum says it's amazing that so many babies are born with nothing wrong. But even if they are perfect, so many diseases and accidents can happen.

Some of the people waiting for transplants were *born* with

heart problems, like me, and some were healthy to start with but at some point caught a virus that damaged their organs, like Precious.

As Mrs Thomas says – you never know what's around the corner in life.

CHAPTER SIXTEEN

DUBIOUS — DOUBTFUL; CAUSING DOUBT; UNCERTAIN; AROUSING SUSPICION
OR DISAPPROVAL
VERNACULAR — BELONGING TO THE COUNTRY OF ONE'S BIRTH; A NATIVE
(USUALLY APPLIED ONLY TO LANGUAGE OR IDIOM); ONE'S MOTHER
TONGUE

MUM ONCE HAD a ginger tom that lived to be twenty. He was saved from drowning at sea by Grandpop. Tiddles was one of a litter that the ship's cook was throwing overboard in a sack. He used to walk round the block following her and Foo the dog (the cat, not Grandpop or the ship's cook). He hated the Pekinese – and hid to pounce and attack him at every opportunity. Tiddles I mean. I giggle at the thought of Grandpop hiding and leaping out to attack the dog. I love when Mum tells me about when she was a child. It's difficult to think of her as a little girl when I know she has grey hair and wrinkles and her body is falling apart. She hates growing old, she says – bits falling off. I resist the temptation to say that I wish I might be able to grow old. Actually I don't really. Who would look after me?

Beelzebub runs to me as soon as I open the bedroom door and runs up my legs as if I'm a tree trunk. Her purr is getting very loud. I have bought her a toy mouse that rattles when she pats it. She was very dubious about it at first and backed away, but when I threw it to her she leapt up and caught it. Instinct. She growls at it like a dog. She was a tightrope walker in another life, I'm sure, as she doesn't like to walk on the floor. Instead she tiptoes around on the chest of drawers, the shelves, bed, chairs, curtain rails and tops of the blinds. I take her outside into the garden to have the first touch of grass under her paws. She watches a blackbird flit in and out of the bushes, her teeth chittering in excitement. I have seen no sign of her *Mutti*. Poor thing, I hope she's all right. Beelzebub sniffs at something fascinating on the grass and does that funny thing that cats do – lifts her top lip and wrinkles her nose as if she's sneering. She is *flehming*. *Flehmen* is a German word for which there is no translation. Cats have an extra organ for scenting, other than their nose. It's called a Jacobson's organ. When they open their mouth and inhale it maximises the number of scent particles that get to the Jacob's organ for analysis and relays the information to the very small brain. I read that in a book called *A Cat is Watching*, written by Roger A Caras, that I found in the second-hand bookshop in Flask Walk. What a clever cat – she has had a wee on the earth. 'Yes, Bubba, it's a large litter tray, especially for you.' There's a blustery wind; I am taking her in, though she spits and folds back her ears when I pick her up.

Dad is coming over and bringing food. It will be like when we all lived together.

It wasn't. Or maybe it was. They had a row because he forgot to buy pears and the *Guardian*. More importantly, he forgot to replenish her whisky supply. She had to drink wine instead. So what? I don't think she should be so critical when we are depending on him to look after us at the moment. We want to watch *Gone With the Wind* again but Daddy refuses, says it's a girlie movie, so we end up watching *Bringing Up Baby*. It's still hilarious after four viewings, but Daddy doesn't watch it to the end. He goes back to the Snow Queen. Masochist! After he's gone, we release Beelzebub from her luxury prison and she watches Baby the leopard in the movie with us. We lie together feet to feet on the three-seater sofa under a double duvet, with another underneath. Beelzebub must think she's in Heaven, not Hell, which is where the original Beelzebub lives.

I have saved a white furry moth from probable death by kitten. It must have come in the window last night but was very well disguised as part of a muslin curtain. Daddy has blinds *and* floaty muslin curtains. I don't think it's an ermine moth, but it might be. It is small and plump bodied – its body lemon yellow with an orange bottom, wings white and legs and head parts hairy as if it wears a white fur coat. I am going to the library tomorrow to find more books on moths and butterflies. You can't have too many books about insects. There's a wonderful one in the local bookshop that has buttons on the front cover, that, when you press them, buzz like a bee or whine like a mosquito.

I'd like to buy it but I suppose it's a bit young for me. Maybe I could buy it for Gabriel. He'd love it. I could take it home as a present to him for looking after my cats.

Beelzebub has struck again – this time she has made a big tear in the black mosquito net over Daddy's bed. I caught her in the act, tangled up and scratching her way out of it. A black kitten tangled in a black net. I took a photo before I rescued her. Does that mean I'm heartless? Maybe I could be a war photographer – dispassionate behind my lens? Oh shit, can I mend it? Can I replace it? How can I hide it? In the end I have to tell Mum and she sews it together for now, ties it in a knot, and says she'll have to see if she can find another.

'Trust your father to have a black one – bloody poseur.'

With luck, he'll never untie it and see the holes, or perhaps he'll think he's got moths. Mum has confiscated the cashmere scarf from Bubba's box. She was quite cross about it. And the clock. So Beelzebub now shares my bed. She sits on the pillow and murmurs into my ear. I realise that Mum finds it quite difficult to be angry with me PT. And I find it difficult to be horrid to her PH (Post Hysterectomy). She is rather weepy still, but looking better than she did in hospital.

In the morning I find a piece of black thread on my pyjamas. I do what Grandma showed me – let the thread float to rest on the floor. It will fall into the shape of the first letter of the name of the boy you like best. There – it's a 'b' or maybe a 'p'. Or a mirror image of a 'p' or a 'b'. How confusing. It's only a silly game anyway.

Because it's a sunny morning, after all my boring tests and drugs and filling in the log, I go outside with Beelzebub and while I'm not watching she disappears. I search under the bushes and peer into the trees but I think she climbed over the fence into the next garden. I call her and call her but she doesn't come. Mum goes next door but there's no one in and she can't get to the back garden. I am frantic. Where is she?

'She'll come when she's hungry,' says Mum.

'But she'll get lost. She hasn't been out of the garden before.'

Clouds cover the sky and it's suddenly cold so we have to close the door. I am so worried, I telephone Willy and ask him to look out of his back window for her but he doesn't see her. Of course, he can't see very well, I forgot.

Daddy arrives, carries out full dustbin bags, brings shopping in. Hoovers. Cleans the bathroom and kitchen. He has lifted the heavy pots and pans down from high shelves to worktop height so Mum doesn't have to stretch or lift them far. He is like a male au pair. I did have an au pair, once, or rather, Mum had. Kyoko, Japanese. I apparently made her life hell. She wasn't the least bit interested in looking after me, though. All she did was bow and smile at Daddy and feed him homemade sweets. She made me fried bread with sugar on. It worked a treat: stopped me bawling. Not too good for my teeth, however. Mum got rid of her and gave up her freelance work to look after me full-time.

What if Bubba finds her way back to Daddy's garden while he's here? What will I do? I lurk by the patio door looking for her.

'Didn't you have a cleaner?' Mum asks Daddy.

'Yes, had to let her go.'

'Yeah?

'Yeah, had a thing about me. You know, unwelcome attention.'

'What? Unwelcome? I don't believe it. Wasn't she pretty enough for you?'

'Ugly as sin, as a matter of fact, but she seemed to think she was some exotic flower that I couldn't wait to pluck. Russian girl. Shame, she was a good cleaner. Eyebrows met in the middle. Scared me shitless.' Mum and I are rolling about laughing, while Daddy looks quite glum. 'Haven't had time to find another yet.' Poor Daddy, he does have women problems.

He's gone. I dress in my winter woollies, go out again and call my kitten but she is nowhere to be seen. I feel so guilty. I should have watched her; she's too adventurous.

'Beelzebub! Bubba, there you are, you naughty little kitty. Come here.' I pick her up and take her inside.

'What's she got in her mouth?' Bubba is looking smug and confused and as if she is trying not to open her mouth. Mum feels inside and brings out a tiny goldfish – no bite marks, but badly sucked. 'Good heavens! Where on earth…? I'll put it down the lavatory.'

'No Mum, it might be alive.'

'It can't be.'

'Let's put it in water, just in case.'

We pour water into my bathroom washbasin and put the fish into it. After floating on its side for about a minute it suddenly quivers and starts swimming, first on its side, but eventually it recovers fully and swims the right way up.

'Ohmygod, Mum, it worked.'

Now I have two creatures to hide from Dad. Where can I keep a fish? What do they eat? How am I going to explain how a live goldfish got here? Will he believe that a fish eagle escaped from the zoo and flew over his garden and dropped it? Or a heron, yes a heron would be more believable, or I won it at a fair on the Heath. Daddy won't have noticed that there isn't a fair there at the moment.

'It must have come from a garden pond,' says Mum.

'I suppose. Couldn't we keep it for Daddy?'

'No, and don't you touch it, either. Remember in the cardiac transplant leaflet? Fish carry disease and you have to wear gloves to handle them.'

'Gloves?' I imagine woolly gloves.

'Rubber gloves, silly.'

Mum says she'll ask the neighbours if they've lost a fish. It's too cold now for me to go banging on doors and, anyway, she says, she has no idea what maniacs might be living in the street. She puts the fish into a plastic bowl and sets off. Ten minutes later, she's back, triumphant. 'It was two doors away, a pond in the back garden. Lovely woman called Lily. She's lost ten this year.'

'Ponds?'

'Goldfish, stupid.'

'Maybe Beelzebub's mother took the rest?' I say. 'And she's inherited a taste for them.' I give her a generous ration of pilchards in tomato sauce for her tea. She purrs in appreciation. 'What a clever naughty wicked thief you are Bubba.'

I have another read of the cardiac transplant leaflet to see if Mum's right about fish. She is. Also, it says to beware of cats and dogs because of animal-carried diseases and to have animals checked by a vet before you go home to them. Oh bloody hell, there's all these new problems come with my new organs. I'll let Mum worry about them. I've got enough worries. No way am I giving up cats.

Now that Bubba's back I can go to the library. In *Eyewitness Insects* I've found an interesting item on moths in Australia. I wonder if Brett knows about it?

In the Bogong mountains of New South Wales, moths are collected from rock crevices and cooked in hot sand. The aborigines remove the heads, grind the bodies into a paste and bake them as cakes. Then they have a feast. The moths provide valuable fat to their diet.

Another fascinating fact: the Indian moon moth has the most acute sense of smell of any insect. It can detect the pheremones of a mate from a distance of eleven kilometres. I must remember to tell people that. I think it's interesting but it could be a great conversation stopper. I'm not very good at conversation.

I haven't had much practice as I only seem to hang around with Mum or other old people these days. I don't really know how to communicate with people my own age. I get the feeling that Summer thinks I'm like… I don't know… an alien or something. When I go back to school things will change, I hope.

I'll take note of the language, the argot, the slang. I think kids still say 'cool' anyway.

Willy, Mum and I walk together on the Heath or up to

Hampstead most days, to the second-hand bookshop when it's not pouring with rain and to his allotment sometimes for tea and biscuits. I've bought him three china mugs with smiley faces on. We're an odd looking trio. Very English eccentric – except that Willy is German. We walk into a flock of pigeons feeding on breadcrumbs. They rise in a tumult of applause around our heads. Mum says it reminds her of sheets cracking in the wind on our washing line in St Ives, and she can almost smell them – her favourite sound and smell. My favourite sounds are of waves shifting sand and gulls wailing. My favourite smell is of seaweed and Charlie's fur. I ask Willy what his favourite smell is and his favourite sound.

'A single malt whisky poured into a cut-glass tumbler. It sounds and smells like the epitome of Bliss.'

'Ah, yes,' says Mum, 'I go along with that.'

Before my transplant, I saw everything as if for the last time. I drank life greedily, wanting to gulp at every sensation, every experience. I was packing it all in, like speed-reading. Now, what's the difference? I see things as they are, but they are brighter, more vivid, because they are mine for a little longer. Precious but sad. I can gaze on a tree full of rooks and see how they are tattered coats, folded umbrellas, hunched witches, and love them because they are a gift to my senses. I have had a reprieve, like someone on death row. I have been moved to another cell, further away from the electric chair, where I can see daylight for the first time. I can take a little more time to savour the sounds, smells, tastes and sights of everyday life, knowing I have a limited time to enjoy them. It's not sad, exactly, but poignant.

POIGNANT: TOUCHING, PATHETIC, ACUTELY PAINFUL, PIQUANTE

Home-made card with picture of seagull and *Get Well Soon* in a heart:

> *Der Gussy,*
> *My puppy is groing big and runs farst. She likes*
> *Trejer [Treasure, the cat] and sleeps with her. I am*
> *bilding a neeu tree hows for yu. Cum soon,*
> *Love,*
> *Gabriel x*
> *PS I fownd my taran... torren... tran... spider. It was*
> *in the erring cuberd. Phaedra fownd it. She screemd*
> *very lowddly. Moss sez I hav to giv it bak to Billy.*
> *But Billy has lost the snake so I wownt. Claire woent*
> *cum in my room enny mor.*
> *Xxx see yu soon.*

Home-made card with drawing of Charlie asleep on a chair:

> *Dearest Gussie,*
> *I hope your recovery is swift and you are feeling*
> *stronger each day. We are all looking forward to*
> *seeing you and your mother again soon. Claire says*
> *you look so bonny. What a shame your homecoming*
> *has been delayed. Such bad luck. But, do not worry,*
> *your cats are well and happy, though I am sure they*
> *are missing you. I have started a painting of them in*
> *their various sleeping places. Rambo is very elusive*
> *though, and hides. I think he is intimidated by the*
> *sheer size of the family and its livestock, especially*
> *the rabbits. My own cat is still banished from the*
> *garden due to her recently acquired taste for chicks.*
> *The surviving chicks are rapidly becoming pullets and*

the cockerel bullies them fussily. Phaedra is enjoying
sixth form college and has joined a rock group – she
the drummer, and Troy is studying for exams. Surf
has been perfect lately, he says and he is missing it.
They both send love,
Looking forward so much to your return,
Give my love to your mother,
With lots of love,
Fay.

A home-made card with drawing of Spike smiling:

Dear Gussie,
When are you coming home? I can't wait. Our
kitten, Spike, is growing up. He prefers me to you
know who and sleeps on my bed. Siobhan has a new
boyfriend – Leo. He's sixteen and has long hair and
tattoos. She wants a tattoo on her shoulder but Mum
won't let her. I want my hair cut like yours. I got a
gold star at school for my English. We had to write a
news item for the school newspaper. I wrote a story
about you and your operation. I've kept it for you to
read.
lol,
From your bestest friend in the whole world – Bridget
xxxxxxx
The school newspaper article:

NEW ORGANS FOR MY FRIEND

GUSSIE STEVENS IS MY NEW BEST FRIEND. SHE IS
OLDER THAN ME, 12, BUT SHE WAS NOT EXPECTED
TO LIVE VERY MUCH LONGER BECAUSE SHE WAS BORN

WITH A BADLY DESIGNED HEART AND LUNGS, AND
SHE COULD NOT BREATHE PROPERLY, SO SHE COULD
NOT RUN OR CLIMB. SHE HAS HAD A VERY LONG AND
COMPLICATED OPERATION IN LONDON TO REPLACE
HER DISEASED HEART AND LUNGS. SHE IS RECOVERING
AND SOON WILL BE COMING TO THIS SCHOOL SO SHE
WILL BE LIKE ANY OTHER GIRL, AND *WE MUST ALL* BE
KIND TO HER BECAUSE SHE HAS HAD A VERY *DIFFICULT*
TIME. SHE LIKES ALL ANIMALS AND INSECTS AND ISN'T
AFRAID OF ANYTHING, EVEN SPIDERS AND BEETLES.
SHE HAS THREE CATS, FLO, CHARLIE AND RAMBO, AND
IS A BIRD-WATCHER. SHE IS ALSO A POET. I THINK
EVERYONE BEFORE THEY DIE SHOULD DONATE THEIR
HEALTHY ORGANS TO SICK PEOPLE SO THAT THEY CAN
HAVE A CHANCE OF LIVING A NORMAL LIFE.

SIGNED – BRIDGET HEANEY

 I write back straight away to say what a good article it is
and to tell her about Beelzebub. Bridget and I both have
black kittens now – if I am allowed to take her home with
me.
 I send a card to Fay, also, thanking her for the felt bag
and telling how much my kitten likes it. I hope she doesn't
mind.

CHAPTER SEVENTEEN

DAPPER—QUICK; LITTLE AND ACTIVE; NEAT; SPRUCE

DAPPERLING—A DAPPER LITTLE FELLOW

APT—FIT; SUITABLE; PROMPT; QUICK-WITTED; LIKELY

DADDY HAS GONE away – Paris I think. I still haven't had a chance to have a go with his laptop and now he's taken it with him. He doesn't have a clue about the kitten.

Mimi, *The Italian Job*, from Mum's designer days, who I have met once before, has come to stay for a week or so. She sleeps on the sofa and Mum sleeps in the big bed with me and Beelzebub. The sick bay, we call it. Mimi is a three times widow – which means she has been married three times and all her husbands have died. She's fiftyish – the same age as Mum. She teeters on stilettos, wears glinting rings on every finger, cooks great pasta and is teaching me how to make sauces. She's taught me Bolognese, Marinara, and basic tomato. There's good deli close by where we can get lovely Parmesan cheese. It's all we seem to eat these days – pasta. I'd like roast chicken, or a chicken pie like Claire makes, or sausages and mash, or mussels and chips. (I'm not allowed shellfish ever again, though.) But Mum and *The Italian Job* prefer to spend more time wine-tasting than cooking.

We invite Willy down to supper and he kisses Mimi's glittering hand and she giggles as if she likes it, even though he must be nearly a hundred years old. Mimi wears a low-neck fluffy fuchsia pink jumper. Mum always says if you've got it, flaunt it. But when will I have it? Will I ever have it? Willy brings champagne and they drink three bottles. That's one each. I have my favourite – elderflower.

'What's that blue stone, Mimi?' I think I can recognise diamonds and rubies but that's about it.

'It's Tanzanite, Gussie, a very rare stone, found only in one place in Africa, in the shadow of Mount Kilimanjaro. A gift from a Kenyan lover – a man who knew all about big cats. Beauty, isn't it?'

Mum and Mimi smile at each other and Mimi winks at me.

'How romantic,' I say. The cut stone is ultramarine blue with a slight hint of purple. A new one for my colour chart – Tanzanite Blue.

'And this one is a fire opal from a geologist who lives in the Yukon.' The stone looks as if there is fire in its blue green heart. Mimi looks wistful as she twists the ring on her little finger. 'And this little cluster is from a Yankie fighter pilot I met during the Vietnam War. And my other opal is from an Aussie croc hunter. Dickhead, he was.'

'Don't believe everything she says,' says Mum, and Mimi raises her eyebrows at me.

'May I look, my dear?' *The Italian Job* gives Willy her hand and he smiles approvingly and takes out a little magnifier from his pocket. 'Charming.' He raises her hand to his lips and kisses it again.

'What happened to your three husbands, Mimi?'

'Don't be rude, Guss.'

'No, sorright, darl, no worries.' She is becoming more Oz as the evening goes on. ''S a long story.' She pours herself another glass of wine. 'A long, sad story. The first one – Arnie – he was an Aussie, died on the job.'

'Mimi…?' Mum's eyes widen.

'Trucking, poor man. I was nineteen. Gutted.'

'What about the second one?'

'Charlie? Oh Charlie… was my darling.' She begins to

sing and Mum shushes her. 'Fifty to my twenty-five, but oh could he dance. Died of a heart attack. Only married two years.' She takes another glug from her glass. 'I was very unhappy until I met Johann. Dutch – big yacht. Big car, big head, big everything. What a berk he was.' She pours them all more wine. 'And well, poor old Johann's liver gave out on him. Poor sod. Hah! Less said about him the better. Big emerald, though!' She waves a hand in the air before wiping her eyes with her paper napkin and then blowing her nose loudly on it. Willy takes her hand and kisses it yet again.

Enough's enough, already. I'm going to bed.

Mimi is taking Mum out to have her hair done. I am staying home with Beelzebub. It's pouring with rain. Willy looks in but is disappointed when he sees that Mimi isn't here and goes away when I insist that I am going to rest. I doze – what a nice word – reading my cat behaviour book. Beelzebub snores in my ear. She has this thing about my hair – licks it. Maybe she likes the taste of the gel I use for the spikes, or perhaps she is being affectionate, or maybe I remind her of her mother. Yeah – a scruffy mangy stray. I've made sure she hasn't been on any more fishing trips.

Mum and *The Italian Job* come home looking great. Mum's hair has turned dark reddy brown and is much shorter than before with a side parting so there is a wing of hair over one eye. It suits her. The grey bits have gone. They also went shopping in Hampstead and are trying on their 'bargains and investments' while I cook supper. I am inventing a sauce tonight – roasted aubergine with sun-dried tomatoes, anchovies and olives. The aubergines were left over from yesterday, the tomatoes and olives were from the deli, and I find a jar of anchovies in the cupboard, so there's very little work to do. I mix them all up and add garlic and balsamic vinegar and threw some basil leaves in at the end – over the spaghetti. Mum and Mimi are dressed to the nines. Where does that expression come from? Mimi says I must have Italian blood, and so I speak with an Italian accent for the rest of the evening.

'It was beauty this arvo, Lara. We oughta do it more often.'

'Yeah cobber,' says Mum, getting into the swing of things Aussie. They get very silly and giggly on red wine and me ditto on Cola. Mimi brings out the best in Mum. Makes her relax and enjoy herself.

I go to bed early with Bubba and Rena Wooflie – mustn't neglect *her*. It is good to see Mum looking and acting human again. I didn't hear her mention her bowels once today – a record.

Mimi takes Mum and me to the hospital for my last two-weekly biopsy. It's nearly three months since my transplant. I have been very lucky to have only had two complications so far. Acute rejection of transplanted tissue happens mostly in the first year, so that's why I have to have regular checks. But now I only need a biopsy once a month, so I won't have to be near the hospital all the time.

It is reassuring to see other post-transplant patients who are doing well and awful when they become sick and have to go back into hospital for treatment. Judy, she's in her twenties, had her transplant when she was eighteen and she's since had a baby. She looks great and her baby is very sweet and absolutely healthy. She comes back for check-ups once a year only, and occasionally to give talks to people waiting for a transplant. Saul, he was fifteen, died after kidney failure. I am one of the lucky survivors. Two babies, who were very ill, couldn't survive long enough to get donor hearts. Half the people waiting for transplants die before a donor is found.

The transplant unit is a strange mixture of joy and sorrow.

Precious arrives and I feel happy again, carefree. I had forgotten how tall he is, and how hunky. We don't talk for long as they split us up for various tests, but I catch sight of him before we leave and blow him a kiss, and he smiles his piano-key smile – the white keys, not the black ones.

The grey hospital grass has turned green. I would like to give all the patients birdfeeders to hang outside their windows. It would cheer them, I think. Perhaps I'll leave them enough money in my will to always be able to feed birds. I do have about a hundred pounds in my bank account, from when Grandpop and Grandma died.

The doctor says I am allowed to go home to Cornwall. Yippee!

On her last day, Mimi drives me to Camden Town to get my hair trimmed and buys me a beautiful white duffle jacket from the market. Mum says she shouldn't have, but I love it. It's a bit big on the shoulders, but I'll grow into it.

I'm sorry to say goodbye to Mimi, she's been such good fun. She's promised to come and visit us in Cornwall.

I think I might write a book of recipes made from leftovers. Mum has invented some interesting meals using leftovers: curries and soups and stir-fries, mostly – like a soup made out of cauliflower cheese and potato-pie leftovers, and another of leftover curried hake and coconut milk. She has bought a new baking tray for Daddy. For some reason she didn't like the idea of roasting food in the old one after the kitten has used it as a litter tray. Bubba now goes outside after each meal and performs. She's a fast learner.

'Mum, can we keep Bubba, please?'

'How can we, Gussie? Three cats are more than enough.

It's expensive to keep them in food and flea injections and flu injections… and she'll need to be spayed and micro-chipped. No, I think we should give her to Willy.'

'*Free Willy*?'

'Don't start that again.'

'I was thinking of calling him *Willy Wonka*, but *Free Willy* suits him much better.'

'It's in very poor taste, darling, so please don't do it. Anyway – the kitten: she'll be company for him. He's a lonely man, you know.'

'I think he'd rather have *The Italian Job*.' I say.

'Gussie!'

So we invite Willy again for a drink and ask him if he would like to have Beelzebub.

'My dears, I would love to have her, but you know I am nearly eighty-three. How long will I live? The poor kitty would get fond of me and then – *kaput!* – I will die. No, that is not fair for her, *nicht war*? And you know, I would fall over her all the time with my stick. And my beautiful Staffordshire figures? She would knock them down. *Nein, nein, nein*. I really cannot have this kitty.'

I can see that he is thinking up excuses and he isn't a cat person at heart. He really doesn't want her. Mum understands and doesn't push it. Goody, we'll have to take Beelzebub home with us.

'Would you perhaps give me your friend's telephone number, my dear Lara? I seem to have mislaid it. She has left something at my apartment.'

'Mimi?

'Yes, the charming *jolie-laide*. One of her many rings.'

'Really? Mum's eyes widen in interest. 'I'll write it down for you.'

Later, Mum says she had no idea that Mimi had been to

Herr Weinberger's flat.

'What's a jolly led, Mum?'

'*Jolie laide*. It means a woman who is not conventionally pretty but interesting and unusual looking, more or less. It's French.'

Perhaps that's what I am – *jolie laide*.

Willy looks very dapper lately, come to think of it. He has trimmed his beard and hair, and looks pleased with himself – a dapperling! It must be spring. I wonder why she took off her rings? Was she doing his washing up? Cleaning his bath? Mum doesn't wear rings, not even her wedding ring any more.

Mum is feeling stronger today, she says. It has been three weeks since she came out of hospital and five weeks since her operation.

The deliveryman has a coffee now when he comes with our groceries. He's called Sid – well he's actually called something else but it's too difficult to pronounce or remember so he says to call him Sid. Mum has a coffee pot on when she knows he's coming so he can't refuse. She flirts outrageously with him, even though he's half her age. She asks him if he's heard of a writer called William Saroyan, who was Armenian-American, apparently, but he hasn't. She's such a know-it-all. I'd never even heard of Armenia. It's good to see her looking cheerful.

I take Bubba outside and sit on the steps with her pretending I'm Audrey Hepburn in *Breakfast at Tiffany's*. I sing 'Moon River' to her and call her Cat but she scampers into the bushes and a blackbird hurries away, sounding its alarm note. I'm afraid she's going to be a good hunter: I better get her a collar with a bell on it.

Mum comes out.

'Mum, do you ever see clouds that look like clouds – not like hippos or volcanoes or Alsation dogs or horrible faces?'

'Yeah – that one there. It's a Cumulus Gigantus.'

'I knew that.'

'Course you did.'

'Where's Armenia, *Mutti*?'

She tells me the story of the destruction of practically the entire Armenian population by the Turks. It wasn't all that long ago – the first part of the twentieth century, a genocide even before the Holocaust. Millions of people slaughtered. I don't understand why we are so terrible to each other. It's as if people suddenly go mad and start killing anyone who is different from them. But we are all human and ought to be able to live together by now. It's obvious no one is ever going to be able to absorb the amount of history we need to not make mistakes in the future. How do teachers decide what to teach children? I suppose, though once you have learned to read, the rest is up to you. If you want to know things you can look them up in books and libraries and archives, whatever.

Who was my donor? 'Female, under twenty.' It's like the epitaph for an unknown soldier. She could have been a beautiful young woman, a university student who died in a car crash after a party; an actress; a young mother who stepped off the pavement with her baby in a buggy in front of a bus. Has she a boyfriend or husband who is mourning for her? What happened to the baby? Her parents must be feeling dreadful. But at the same time, they will have the consolation of knowing that their daughter's heart and lungs are helping someone have a longer life. Will they be aware that I have survived this far? I expect they do know. If it was my daughter who had died, I'd be glad her organs were still being used – my blood pumping through her heart, my breath filling her lungs. How weird and wonderful! They might have donated her corneas and her kidneys as well. Her organs could be helping several people, not just me. Should I give her a name? I feel I should. It would be like having an imaginary friend. I think I'll give her an ordinary girlie name, not like my own awful name. Augusta, Ugh!

List of names I like:
Susannah (graceful lily)
Hannah (graceful one)
Estelle (a star)
Grace (graceful, attractive one)
Flora (flower) Better not have this one as I'll get confused with Flo.
Josephine (female version of Joseph – increaser, whatever that means. I suppose it means he had lots of children.)
Annabelle (graceful, beautiful)
Daisy (eye of the day, small sun)
Madeleine (elevated, magnificent)
Beatrice (she who makes people happy)

That's the one. She's made me and my family happy. So, welcome Beatrice, to my life. Bee for short. Be. That's very apt.

Ohmygod, I'd forgotten about Bubba.

'Bubba, Bubba, Bubba, Kitty, Kitty Kitty!'

She appears from nowhere, my little black ghost, chirruping with pleasure, her little tail held high. Oh no! What's she got this time? It's a mouse and she's taken it inside.

'Come here puss, come here,' I ask her nicely and she drops the mouse, which is only sucked rather badly; I can't see any puncture marks. I think Beelzebub's teeth aren't as sharp as an adult cat's teeth. The mouse sits still and the kitten loses interest. However, as I try to catch it, it scuttles away under Daddy's desk. The little hunter tries to follow it but the gap is too tight so she crouches instead, peering at it and swiping with a black paw. After a few minutes she gives up jumps up onto the sofa. I whisk her off the pale suede and shut her into the bedroom. A mouse loose in Daddy's flat! I'll have to hope Bubba gets it eventually, or it finds its way out. If it dies from shock I'll smell it. A dead mouse smells like a gas escape. I read somewhere that they actually pee all the time, even when they are running. Mum says she has that problem, but I think she's exaggerating. So wherever it goes the floor will be contaminated. Ugh, it puts me off sitting on the carpet or walking barefoot.

CHAPTER EIGHTEEN

INSIGNIFICANT — DESTITUTE OF MEANING; WITHOUT EFFECT; UNIMPORTANT; PETTY

TYRANT — AN ABSOLUTE RULER; A RULER WHO USES HIS POWER ARBITRARILY AND OPPRESSIVELY; AN OPPRESSOR; A BULLY

PRECIOUS IS COMING to see me. We have bought cakes and pastries from the patisserie and Mum has found some South African tea – Red tea or something – that she thinks his Mum might appreciate. It's called *Rooibos*, which means Red bush. I have made some scones and we have Cornish clotted cream and strawberry jam to go with them – must introduce Precious to our traditional food. I wonder if he'd like Cornish pasties?

'Hi, Presh.' We hug and he shakes Mum's hand. He is very old fashioned and charming and Mum loves it. He is as tall as her and looks totally different without his dressing gown. Normal. He's wearing a white hoodie, a fake fur hooded parka, a woollen scarf and woolly gloves, jeans and probably thermal underwear, though I don't ask. His feet are huge, in leather sneakers. He has a cough, which I worry about. Is it significant? Does it mean he is ill? He assures me he is fine. Mum and Agnes sit and chat and we have tea and cake. Beelzebub is being naughty, as usual, tearing around the back of the sofa and leaping onto our heads. Agnes is scared of him – scared of a kitten! And she's from a country that has lions and leopards, though maybe that's why she's frightened. So she is banished to the bedroom – Beelzebub of course, not Agnes. Let's hope the mouse doesn't appear. I expect she'd have forty fits (a Grandma expression).

Precious has never been on Hampstead Heath. It's cold and windy but bright and sunny. Daffodils are everywhere in the little front gardens on the edge of the Heath.

'Are you running yet?' I ask.

'No, but I'm working out at a gym, to rebuild muscle. I lost lots.' He still whispers.

'Yeah. Well, you're looking good. How do you feel?' He looks hunky actually,

'Yeah, good, good.' He towers over me and I feel rather insignificant.

'What's happening with your family in Zimbabwe?'

He shakes his head and doesn't reply.

'Oh, I'm sorry... Look, the swans!' A black swan has joined an ordinary white one on the pond. He must have escaped from Regent's Park or somewhere. He is the negative and the other the positive, each one with small fierce head held high, strong neck proudly curved, the powerful wings folded and neat, and we cannot see the scaled legs and webbed feet under the green water. Bloody hell, I forgot the camera.

'The thwans are like uth,' Precious says, beaming.

The white swan leans her head to the black swan and their beaks meet in a caress. I feel light-headed, dizzy; something twists in my belly.

I tell him about the mouse and he says I'm right, his mother would have a fit if she knew, and he laughs loud, jumping up and down in glee. He grabs my hands and makes me jump with him, then he starts running and drags me with him, and I'm laughing and nearly wetting myself. And he twirls me in a circle around him, the white crisp grass crackling under my red DMs, his huge sneakers. We are laughing and laughing, carefree as a couple of kids, and the sulking rooks peer down in amazement at us and fly off together, squawking to a quieter tree.

'Let's get back, Gussie, you look cold.' I don't tell him I feel warm inside, warm and happy and excited. He wraps his arm around my shoulders and we walk, my steps enormous to keep up with him. I'm enveloped in his bigness and strength. I wonder whose heart he has under his ribs? I don't ask if he has a name for his new heart. He has more important things to think about: his father and sisters; their future; his home, his health.

I can't wait to go to school and start learning about the world – politics and stuff (as Phaedra would call it). Why doesn't someone do something about Robert Mugabe? He's insane, isn't he? Shouldn't he be locked up and looked after, given drugs to cure him? His people are suffering for his illness, he isn't. Or is he a tyrant? Mum would say he is. An evil tyrant who is torturing, starving and killing his own countrymen, and everyone is suffering because of his actions. What do you do with someone like that? Don't look at me, how should I know? I'm only twelve. The trouble is he is also destroying the life of my friend and his family.

'What do you think will happen in Zimbabwe?'

'I don't know.'

'Won't the people rise up and destroy the bad government?'

'How can they fight against guns?'

I hadn't thought about that. I suppose sticks and stones aren't going to win any battles.

After they left, Mum told me what Agnes had said: that her husband has changed his mind. He now feels he must stay in Zimbabwe and help in the only way he knows. He's a doctor and that's what doctors do. Nearly everyone who can, is leaving – those with money abroad, or friends or relations who would sponsor them. He feels he must stay to help care for those who are too sick to care for themselves. Their farmer friends were ditching all their belongings and getting out, with no money. Most of his Zimbabwean doctor colleagues have already gone to Australia, New Zealand, Canada or South Africa.

'But my daughters?' Agnes had asked. 'They will stay with me,' he said. 'No. You must send our daughters to England. Get them on a plane.'

He had agreed at last, after a long argument. He'll see if he can get them a flight out.

'Won't you miss him?' Mum asked her.

'He will do what he wants to do. I cannot stop him.' Agnes said.

'But how will they live?' I ask Mum. 'Will Agnes be able to be a doctor in England?'

'God knows, but it's presumably better than trying to live under Mugabe.'

Kalibusiwe Ilizwe Le Zimbabwe. That's the national anthem. Blessed be the Land of Zimbabwe.

CHAPTER NINETEEN

RECONCILE—TO RESTORE OR BRING BACK TO FRIENDSHIP OR UNION: TO
BRING TO AGREEMENT OR CONTENTMENT; TO PACIFY: TO MAKE, OR TO
PROVE CONSISTENT

PROFOUND—DEEP; REACHING TO A GREAT DEPTH; INTELLECTUALLY DEEP;
LEARNED; DEEPLY FELT

MUM AND I and Beelzebub are watching *Les Vacances de M.
Hulot* (*M. Hulot's Holiday*). It's one of my favourite comedy
movies of all time. The trouble is it still hurts when I laugh,
and I can't stop laughing. Jacques Tati's walk is enough to
give me hysterics. I love when the English wife strolls in
front of her husband wittering on about nothing and finding
shells on the beach and he ignores her totally. And when Tati
goes to sea in a kayak that collapses and concertinas into
a shark-fin shape, sending all the swimmers into a panic;
and when he plays ping-pong in the hotel and causes chaos.
And when he accidentally ignites a firework with his pipe;
the ice-cream that threatens forever to topple but doesn't
– so many details that make up a brilliantly hilarious movie.
There's no real dialogue, just music and funny noises, so
you don't need to know French. I really like another of his
movies – *Mon Oncle* (*My Uncle*). Perhaps we'll watch that
another time, when my ribs have stopped aching. It's great
having all Daddy's movie collection to choose from. I'll miss
it when we go home.

I've been thinking about Precious and his family. If his
father stays in Zimbabwe, but sends Precious's sisters to
England, they will be like me, fatherless. I think Precious is
reconciled to the idea of staying here. He needs the specialist
medical care he'll get in England. He and his mother are living

in West London with relatives. Maybe he could come and stay in Cornwall? We have loads of room. I'll ask Mum.

I have been thinking about the word 'reconcile'. I have an idea. I am going to perform reconciliation between Daddy and Mum. I saw that adoring look she gave him in hospital when he said he would look after us. And after all, it is spring.

He's back but he's reconciled with (or is it to?) the Snow Queen and staying at her place. However, I have a cunning plan...

I wait until *Mutti*'s in the bath. The Snow Queen answers the phone.

'Huh, it's you,' she hisses, and I can see icicles dripping from her nose, blood oozing from iceberg blue eyes. 'I'll get Jackson.' She spits the words like bullets. I stick my tongue out as far as it will go and put a finger to the end of my nose and waggle my fingers.

'Gussie?'

'Daddy, dearest darlingest Daddy.'

'Gussiebun!'

Gussiebun. He used to call me that when I was little. Oh, it makes me feel so... so little and safe.

'Daddy, could you do something for me, please Daddy?'

'Anything, you know that.' I think he's been drinking. Good.

'It's Mum.'

He sighs loudly. 'Tell.'

Mum is reading a paperback Claire left her on How to Be a Better Human Being or something.

'Mum.'

'Sweetheart?' She holds me around the waist as I lean into her.

'Mum, could you do something for me?'

'What is it? You know I'd do anything for you.' She kisses my head. The book is obviously having a profound effect on her. She's on her second whisky. Good.

'It's Daddy.'

She sighs loudly.

'Tell.'

'He told me he'd like to take you out to dinner but didn't think you'd say yes and he can't stand the rejection and he asked me to sound you out.'

'Sound me out!'

'Yes, he would really love to take you out and give you a treat as you've had such a hard time. He wants to take you to a really lovely restaurant.'

'Lovely restaurant?'

'Don't repeat my every word! It makes you sound like a moron.' I think she's hooked. She makes an appointment to have her hair done.

She's taking forever getting dressed. Mimi and I are watching Channel Four News and eating at the same time. Why do they always show starving people or dead people when we do that? It makes me feel sick and guilty. I know it's right to know about the suffering in the world, but it's always when we're eating. Mimi changes the programme. Mum comes in wearing black trousers, a white frilly shirt and boots.

'What about this?'

'Nah.' Mimi doesn't approve. 'Show some leg, darl. You've got great legs. Show your cleavage. Know what they say? If you've got it...'

'Flaunt it.' We all say and laugh.

Daddy rings the doorbell as if he hasn't got a key and this isn't his place. I open the door.

Bubba's secure in my bedroom.

'Honeybun!' He kisses me gently. 'Mimi.' He kisses her cheeks. 'Long time no see.' Mum comes into the room. 'Wow! You look… Wow!' Daddy raises his eyebrows. She wears a black low-necked lacy job with a tight skirt that reaches just above her knees and red high heels. She's had her hair done and wears red lipstick. I've never seen her look so pretty. Well, not pretty exactly, but gorgeous. Younger. She's blushing. They go off like they actually like each other.

Mimi plays Scrabble with me but she's hopeless. Keeps spelling words as if they're Strine (Australian). In the end we spell anyway we like, but have to pronounce the word the way we spell it and lie about its meaning. It's a cool rule and I learn lots of Strine swear words that I can use with Brett.

'Mimi, do you think Mum might get back together with my Daddy?'

'I dunno, Gus. What do *you* think?'

'I don't see why not. He can't possibly love the Snow Queen, can he?'

'Is that the one who looks like she's got ice cubes up her arse?'

I giggle. 'Yes, she's awful.'

'Well, I don't know about your father. I don't know him well. But I know your mother is concerned first and foremost about you and your happiness, sweetheart.'

'I'd be happy if she and Daddy were together again.'

'Yeah, well, darl, I don't know what she'll do. I guess you've just gotta wait and see what happens. You can't force love, you know, Guss. Your go.'

'No, it's yours.'

'Oh, is it? Righto.' She puts down SHONKY on a double word with the Y at the end of PUN to make PUNY.

'What's that mean?'

'Shonky? It means underhanded or devious. Strine.'

'Okay.' She's winning now and loving it. Thank goodness we aren't playing for money.

Then she sees it. 'Eeek! Fuckaduck! It's a rat!'

'It's Bubba's mouse,' I tell her and find a napkin to catch it with. Bubba is stalking it, but the mouse is too quick and hides behind a radiator. I shut the frantic kitten in the bedroom and rescue the mouse. Mimi is standing on the sofa, clutching a glass of wine, her face a picture of horror.

'Open the patio door so I can put it out,' I tell her, and she reluctantly climbs down and opens it. I step out into the cold orange glow of night and let the mouse go onto the earth. I sniff the air and smell the lovely London night scents of diesel, dead leaves, old bricks. There are no stars, just an orange haze.

'Come in and shut the door, for gawd's sake, Guss, it'd freeze the balls off a croc.'

I'll miss London and the people I've met when I go back home. There aren't enough foreigners in Cornwall, except during the summer season.

'Well that was interesting,' Mimi says. Any more livestock to show me?'

I go to bed about ten thirty, leaving Mimi listening to music with Willy, who has appeared with a bottle of champagne.

I wait on tenterhooks (or is it tenderhooks – where does that come from?) for Mum to return. I read one of Daddy's film-making books while Bubba purrs in my ear. When I feel myself dropping off I take off my glasses, plump my pillow and open the window. A taxi draws up, Mum gets out, pays the driver, and comes in. She's alone. I put on my dressing gown. Laughter from the sitting room. Mimi and Willy leaving, I think. I open the door a chink and peer out.

Mutti's sitting alone at the table eating a chunk of cheese and has her fingers in a jar of pickled gherkins. Bubba comes out with me to see what's what and maybe have a little supper. She likes cheese very much, but only if I give it to her with my fingers. Put it on a plate and she turns up her little black nose and runs away offended. Bubba, not Mum.

'Well?'

'Well what? Why aren't you asleep?'

'What happened?'

'Hah! Disaster! Your father is such a… It Wasn't the Best Evening I've Ever had.'

'Wasn't the best evening…? What happened?'

She sighs. 'Well first of all he sets fire to the restaurant.'

'Sets fire to the restaurant?'

'Don't repeat everything I say, please, Gussie, it makes you sound like a moron.'

I smack her lightly on the arm, and giggle.

'Your father,' (she always calls him my father when she's angry with him) 'passed the bread-basket Too Close to the Candle in the middle of the table and the napkin in the basket Caught Fire and bits of Flaming Paper flew all round us.'

'Ohmygod. Is that how you hurt your thumb?' It has a plaster around it.

'No. I'm getting to that. I had grilled lobster. Your father said I could choose anything I wanted. Smart Restaurant, my foot! (Another foot expression for my collection.) 'Not even linen napkins! Paper! Huh! It took me three asks to get a finger bowl. Tried to fob me off with a scented paper packet thingy. Ugh! And they hadn't split the claws properly, and when I was trying to break one open with my hands the shell split my thumb from top to bottom.'

'Ohmygod.'

'Yeah, blood everywhere. Needed more than paper

napkins, I can tell you. That's not all. I went to the cloakroom to clean the cut, having told your father to get a plaster from the waitress. Twenty minutes later I was still running cold water on my cut. Gave Up Waiting. Eventually, wrapped my lacerated thumb in toilet paper and went back to the table. They Hadn't got a First Aid Kit, Can you Believe?'

'Isn't that illegal?'

'Yes. Someone had to go up the street to get a plaster from Another Restaurant. It took Forever.'

'I don't believe it.'

'Believe it. Meanwhile your father's finished his main course, drunk most of the second bottle of My Favourite vino, is tucking into sticky toffee pudding and chatting up the Busty Blonde at the Next Table. Not the Least Bit Concerned. I could have Bled to Death down there. I wasn't Too Happy, I can tell you.'

I could imagine Mum being Not Too Happy with Daddy.

'And to complete a Perfect Evening with Your Father, I find I have lobster juice and garlic butter down the front of my New Frock.' I notice her dress is wet where she has soaked it.

'Oh dear, poor *Mutti*.'

'I'm famished,' she says, her hand stuck in the pickle jar.

'Was that all?'

'All? What do you want? World War Three? No, Actually, it wasn't quite all. I threw the remains of the very nice Chardonnay over your father. There was hardly any in the bottle so I emptied the jug of water over him too. Huh! His face!' She smiles smugly. 'Don't think he'll be welcome there again.'

'Want a wally, sweetie?'

Mum offers me a gherkin.

CHAPTER TWENTY

DISCREET—PRUDENT; CIRCUMSPECT; JUDICIOUS; CAUTIOUS (IN ACTION OR SPEECH)

INCORRIGIBLE—HOPELESSLY BAD OR DEPRAVED; BEYOND ANY HOPE OF REFORM OR IMPROVEMENT IN CONDUCT

MUM'S SWIGGED HALF a carton of orange juice and is doing the Full English thing with bacon, egg, sausage, tomato and fried bread and I'm having porridge, apple-juice and a warm bread roll and honey. I give Bubba her first breakfast of real cat food from a tin and Mum has to go to the bathroom for a while. When she comes out she says she reckons the lobster must have been off and it's poisoned her system. She does look green. She can't face her coffee she says and takes one look at Bubba's food and goes back to the bathroom. It seems her usual method of killing a hangover hasn't worked. She's yet to dose herself with sugar, though. Perhaps I'll take her a hot chocolate in an hour or so.

Bubba is so funny with her tinned food. She acts as if I've insulted her. She spits at it and hisses, her back fluffed up to make herself huge (as big as a slice of chocolate cake). She backs away and shakes her head. Then she creeps towards it as if it's an enemy, her ears back. She puts her nose to the plate and licks tentatively. She sniffs, licks, sniffs. Where's the pilchard? What, no tomatoes? She licks again and she's eating it. She's a proper cat. When she's finished she goes to the door to be let out. It's a cold and blustery wet day, but she runs to the patch of earth at the edge of the patio and gets into a crapping position. It's the only time a cat looks less than beautiful. We once went to the Picasso Museum in Paris. There were all sorts of wonderful paintings and sculptures and pottery there, but the thing I remember best was a life-size bronze cat having a crap. It was by a door, very discreetly placed and looked so real. I looked to see if there was a lump of bronze poo but there wasn't. I tried to find a postcard of it in the shop but failed. I've never seen it in a book either.

I call her to come in and after she has dutifully scratched the earth to cover her poo she rushes in to me. The next ten minutes are spent grooming herself. She still falls over when she's trying to clean her tummy. She's very sweet and I do hope I can keep her. I'm sure Charlie and Rambo will love her when they get to know her. Even grumpy old Flo should be able to tolerate a little kitten on her territory.

Willy comes round to borrow some milk and I tell him about Mum's disastrous dinner. We laugh. He looks rather pleased with himself this morning. He's dressed in paisley patterned silk dressing gown with a yellow silk scarf tucked in at the neck. I think it's called a cravat. He looks like a suave old Cary Grant.

'Will you have a coffee, Willy? There's loads left.'

'*Danke schön*, Gussie, but no. I have a… a very special guest upstairs.'

For breakfast? I think but don't say. I am attempting to be discreet. Mum says I speak my mind too often and should think of other people's feelings.

'Is your *Mutti* here?'

'In the bathroom.'

'Ah yes, of course. You don't have any biscuits to spare, do you, Gussie? Croissants? I haven't done any baking this week. No? Smoked salmon? No? Ach well, never mind. I must go back. I hope your *Mutti* is better soon. You seem to spend your time looking after her, you poor child.' He gives a little skip on his way out.

Thinking about it, he's right. I do seem to be the carer in this family. Am I the only one who cares about keeping the family together? Dad doesn't give a duck's arse (a Mimi expression); Mum's behaviour doesn't help. Perhaps I'll be a counsellor when I grow up. Specialising in marriage bust-ups in families with a transplant member.

I hope this little incident doesn't mean that Daddy won't come to see me. Maybe he'll want us to leave. After all, we're paying no rent, it's his place, and Mum has just assaulted him in public.

What can I do with them both? They're incorrigible. I'm never going to get them back together. I am thinking dark thoughts when the phone rings. Maybe it's Daddy phoning to apologise. Except that I suppose it's Mum who should be saying sorry. I don't know. Why do grown-ups make everything so complicated?

'Oh, it's you.' It's Alistair.

'How are you, Gussie?'

'All right, I suppose.'

'Is your mother there?'

'Yes, but she's in the bathroom. She went out for dinner with Daddy last night.' Why did I say that? It's as if I want to hurt him. And I don't; he's nice. But he's not Daddy. He's only my doctor in Cornwall.

'I see.' I'm sure he doesn't. What does he see?

'When are you coming home, Gussie, do you know?'

'Don't know. Mum hasn't had her final check-up yet.

'How goes your treatment?'

'Boring.' I don't feel like talking to him, I don't know why. Perhaps I feel that if I'm nice to Mum's boyfriend it'll encourage him. I want my Daddy back. Why was Mum so horrid? Why can't she try to behave? She's so selfish. I hate her.

'Is everything okay, Gussie?'

'Yeah, fine.'

'Well, give her my love and say I phoned, won't you.'

'Yeah, okay. Bye.' I put the phone down and run into my room and curl up on the bed with Bubba. There's a horrid tight feeling in my throat, like the awful soreness when the breathing tube was taken out. I swallow tears but my eyes leak in spite of my attempts to feel nothing. Bubba squeaks at me and shoves her little face into mine. I give in to my feelings and let my tears flow.

CHAPTER TWENTY-ONE

MUM GETS TO the phone before I do.

'Right. In that case I'll do some shopping in the village. What time are you arriving?' She puts down the phone. 'Your father will be here at eleven. I'm going out.'

There's just time to sort out Bubba's breakfast and toilet ritual and hide her away before he gets here.

He arrives carrying a large and heavy black portfolio, which he places on the glass-topped dining table.

'Surprise, honeybun.'

He opens the case and peels back tissue paper to expose a large photo print of an old man looking straight at the camera. He has laughter lines splaying from his eyes, a large nose and wears a flat cap. I sort of recognise it and then realise...

'That's mine. I did that in one of the fishermen's lodges.'

Daddy has had some of my black and white photographs printed large on beautiful thick watercolour paper with a black line around them and lots of white border. There are six pictures of the men playing dominoes, laughing, chatting and smoking. There's a print of a woman in a floral wrap-around apron standing against a hedge of valerian.

'That's our neighbour, Mrs Thomas. She's had an eye operation and her cat Shandy has died.' Mum must have given him my exposed film from home.

'I like the hospital pics, very atmospheric.' He's right. They look interesting: Mr Sami in his surgical greens, his mask over his mouth and nose, his eyes tired and sad; the physios looking straight at the camera; a picture of Katy and Soo Yung laughing together. The one I did at the aqua-fit class is amusing, though I don't think Mum will like the way she looks. She always has her mouth open and her eyes closed in photographs. At least she's not holding a drink in this one.

The women are in a circle formation, not unlike my dream of elephants swimming, except of course, the women don't look at all like elephants.

I wonder how the ninety-something-year-old lady is? She was really interesting and I'd like to meet her again. I'd like to hear more about her life. I bet she's had adventures.

There's more. The old negatives that my great-grandfather Amos Hartley Stevens made of St Ives: the harbour full of fishing boats with dark sails, gulls wheeling overhead, and portraits of fishermen and their wives – Daddy's had them made into bronze-grey prints on the same lovely rough paper.

'What's this colour Daddy? How do they do that?

'Selenium toning. Looks great doesn't it?'

'I love it.'

'What do you think about an exhibition, Guss?'

'An exhibition of Amos Hartley Stevens' photographs?'

'Yes, and yours. I think it would make a great show – continuity, family talent, handing on the torch, that sort of thing.'

'My pictures? In an exhibition?' I am so astonished at the idea I can't speak.

'I've talked to the powers that be at the archive. They've okayed it. He was quite a guy, my grandfather. Important in the scheme of things. Yeah.'

'So, the exhibition would be at the film archive?'

'Yeah, the corridor. They do stills exhibits there. If you are okay about if we'll probably schedule it for next winter for a month.

I am so gobsmacked I can't speak. I might even be having a heart attack. I wouldn't know, as a transplanted heart feels no pain. I hug him tight.

'Oh thank you, Daddy, thank you.' He places a hand on my head. I think my heart might actually burst, I am so happy.

CHAPTER TWENTY-TWO

DISPARAGE—TO DECRY; TO BELITTLE; TO LOWER IN RANK OR REPUTATION; TO DEPRECIATE

'I'LL BELIEVE IT when I see it,' said Mum when I told her my news.

'Why do you do that?'

'What?'

'Put him down all the time. He says he'll do it, he'll do it.'

Yes. Okay, maybe he'll keep his word this time.'

Why does she always disparage him? He's trying his best. I think it's lovely that he's gone to so much trouble for me. He's doing it for me. It's his way of showing he cares. He took the large prints with him, for framing, but left me with smaller prints of my pictures, including one of Mum asleep, her mouth open.

She is suitably embarrassed and forbids me to use it in any exhibition ever. In fact she says I should tear it up. But she likes the others.

'They're very good, sweetheart. You're very clever,' she says and I feel a warm glow. I want to tell the world. Instead I phone Claire and tell her. That way, practically everyone I know will get to hear about it.

'Can I phone Brett, please Mum?'

'Go on then, but don't be long.'

'Brett, It's Gussie. I've got exciting news.'

'Hi, Gussie, howyadoin?'

'I'm much better, thanks. You'll never guess – I'm going to have an exhibition of my photographs in London.'

'Goodonya, Guss. That's ripper. When you coming home?'

'Soon, I think. Mum's got to wait a bit longer before she's allowed to travel, then we'll come. Brett, I've got a new kitten.'

'I heard, yeah, from Bridget. How will the other cats get on with it? That'll be a laugh.' I suddenly remember the photo of Bubba caught in the mosquito net. Didn't Daddy see it? Or is it still on the undeveloped film in the Leica?

It's so good to hear Brett's Aussie voice. I can imagine his curly mouth smiling at the phone. 'How are you, Brett? What's happening in St Ives?'

'Not a lot. Went birding with Dad – the starlings at Marazion. Thousands of them go to roost in the marshes. It's a great sight. Wish you could see it. The racket they make!'

I suddenly miss the wide-open skies of West Cornwall, the curve of the bay and the noisy sea. I can almost smell it. And then I hear them, the gulls at his end of the phone. Homesickness hits me like a stab in the chest.

'How are you feeling?'

'Well, thanks. I have to take loads of pills every day and have tests and things, but I'm doing all right. You won't recognise me. I'm pink and I've put on weight.'

'Still got your England cap?'

'Of course.'

'And the red DMs?'

'Yes.'

'Then I'll recognise you.'

'Gotta go, Brett, bye.' I can feel Mum's eyes boring into me.

'See ya, Guss.'

I feel happiness like an orange swirl of colour inside a lava lamp, rising and bubbly, swelling and glowing. Then I feel slightly guilty. It's not really an exhibition of my pictures, but my great-grandfather's images. Still, he doesn't know that. It's my show too. And I haven't mentioned Precious. I should have. It's funny how I feel so happy today, when I felt so sad yesterday. I don't think it's only the drugs. I suppose I am going to have to accept the fact that Mum doesn't want to live with Daddy again. Anyway, I have my own life to lead; the life of a famous photographer. Perhaps I could write poetry in my spare time.

'Gussie, could you put this plaster on for me? I can't do it with one hand.'

'When can we go home Mum?'

'Soon.'

'And will I be able to go to school?'

'We'll see.'

CHAPTER TWENTY-THREE

MAWKISH—LOATHSOME, AS SOMETHING DECOMPOSED OR MAGGOTY; SICKLY SWEET; INSIPID; MAUDLIN

I'VE MADE A list of my exhibition photographs and given them all titles.

St Ives series:
Mrs Thomas
Dominoes
Euchre
No Swearing
Aqua-fit

Hospital series:
View from hospital bed
Heart monitor
Window onto hospital garden
Physiotherapist
Cardiac surgeon
Night nurse
Cardiac nurses

All very simple and straightforward. Daddy says it's best not to give photographs titles like THE NIGHT WATCH; HOPE COMES WITH THE DAWN and stuff like that. It's mawkish and embarrassingly amateurish. So I've stuck to straightforward description. Daddy is having really good frames made. His grandfather's photos and mine are having the same mounts and frames. Ivory mounts and black wood box frames. But it's ages before the exhibition. Nearly a year.

'Phone, Gussie, answer it please.'

I'm grooming my kitten, who is lying on her back enjoying every moment. She is so sweet.

'Okay, Mum, I've got it.'

'Hello. This is the Jackson Stevens residence.' I'd make such a good secretary. There's no answer, though I can hear someone breathing heavily at the other end. 'Who's there?' Whoever it is, is crying I think. 'Hello? Hello?'

'Give it here.' Mum takes the phone from me.

'Hello? Who is that? Agnes? Is that you? What is it? What's happened dear?'

I don't think I can bear it. Precious has died.

CHAPTER TWENTY-FOUR

I THINK ABOUT death quite often. My own death. I expect it will be like before I was born – nothingness, or nothing I can remember. But I prefer to think that my spirit will become something else. I think it might be wonderful to be a bee, busy at my duties each day, building a hive, sipping at nectar, buzzing into the golden hearts of roses or daisies. It would be wonderful just to be a daisy in a meadow, surrounded by buttercups and other daisies, bobbing in the breeze. I would close my petals at night and sleep, and open them each day of my life and worship the sun. Even being grass would be good, but to be a bird would be best. A white gull, skimming waves, riding the winds, swooping and swerving and calling to my mate in the dark; or a skylark ascending, singing my heart out in the blue sky above the hilly dunes, fluttering my wings and hovering over the sand, suddenly diving to my nest hidden in the marran grass.

I think Precious might become a sunflower, his open face following the path of the sun, like a huge smile. Or maybe he has become an African bird – one that has long legs and large feet and glossy feathers. I don't know many African birds apart from sea eagles and toucans as I wasn't very interested in birds when I was in Kenya, which is a terrible waste. If I ever do go back to Africa I'll definitely learn more about them. Glossy Ibis – Precious would make a wonderful Glossy Ibis. I wish I had known him better. I wish he hadn't died.

On the day I am not well enough to go to the funeral. It is icy and wet and so grey the sky never lightens after breakfast time. I stay in bed and Mum administers to me, bringing me hot drinks that I cannot even sip without choking with emotion.

'Scrabble?' she asks. I shake my head. Nothing, I must do nothing today, but think of Precious and his smile that is like a sunflower. I cannot bear to think of his father and sisters in Zimbabwe; his mother alone in England.

'You go, Mum, you should go,' I tell her, but she won't leave me. She's sent flowers – daffodils and Paper Whites, all spring flowers and I wrote a note on a card: '*I will never forget you, Precious friend. Love, Gussie.*'

I have no idea what a Shona funeral is like. His family are Christians, I know that.

'Mum, do they sing hymns, do you think?'

'I expect so, and they pray. There's a Zimbabwean poet – Ignatius Mabasa. He wrote a poem called *Kana Ndafa* which means *When I Die*. It's about the false words in praise of the bereaved that get spoken at Shona funerals.'

'How do you know that?'

'I'm not just a pretty face, you know.'

'Say that again…'

'I'm not just a pretty face.'

'The title.' I smile witheringly at her.

'*Kana Ndafa*.'

'I wish I had learned some Shona from Precious. I didn't ask him anything.'

'We must learn as much as we can, while we can,' she said.

'Yes Mum. I'll try.' We hold each other and weep for Precious and all the other transplant patients we have briefly known and lost. Bubba pushes her head into our faces in sympathy and I hold her, too.

CHAPTER TWENTY-FIVE

MUM HAS BEEN to the Royal Free for her final check-up. We're going home. Alistair can't take time off to come for us and Daddy is away, inevitably, so we're going by train. I like trains, anyway. I can read and watch the world fly by and play Scrabble with Mum. And I love to eat egg sandwiches for lunch.

We get a cardboard pet-carrier from the pet shop and we fill up the birdfeeders in Daddy's garden with seed and nuts. I leave written instructions for Daddy on how often to fill the feeders and to wash them regularly in disinfectant. Poor Mr Robin, I probably shouldn't have tried to tame him. It's probably my fault he was killed. I've left a going-away-thank-you present for Daddy – a blue tit nesting box, but neither of us can reach to nail it on the copper beech. I do hope he fixes it in the right place. It needs to be over six feet off the ground, not facing direct sun, away from cats and with branches nearby so the birds have cover when they fly to and from their nestlings.

Bubba has breakfast and I take her out for what I hope will be her only poo of the day until we get home. I think of poor Mr Robin and hope another one will soon claim his territory. Bubba does a quick tour of the garden, climbs the fence at the end to look for goldfish and I grab her and put her in the travel box.

Mimi has come to see us off and she and Willy help us carry our luggage from the flat to the taxi, though the cases have wheels so they only have to carry them down the steps. The driver lifts the cases into the boot. Beelzebub comes with me into the cab and I talk to her all the time so she won't be frightened by all the strange noises and motion.

'Are you sure we can't come with you to help at Paddington?' Mimi asks.

'We'll be fine, really.'

'Don't forget, Lara, what I said about freelancing. You could do it, darl.'

'No, I won't forget.' They kiss. 'Wow, is that a new ring?'

Mimi smiles like the Cheshire cat and flashes her diamond ring at us.

'My engagement ring from Willy,' she says and squeezes his arm. He's shaved off his beard. He looks very happy and ten years younger – no, twenty years younger. Smiles do that sometimes.

'You must come for the wedding my dears. In three months – June.'

'Plan it to coincide with one of Gussie's check-ups, then.'

'Of course.'

'Goodbye Willy, it has been so lovely to get to know you.' Mum gives him Daddy's keys. He hugs us both and kisses Mum's hand.

'It has been a privilege to know you both,' he says. I cry. I'm no good at goodbyes. He brushes away a tear. Mimi blows her nose loudly. I wish Daddy could have been here.

We get the driver to help with the bags and Beelzebub's box at the other end. Mum has found out how many children he has in Iran and when he came to London, and if he likes it here, so when we leave him he is smiling and waving to us like an old friend. She'd phoned ahead for passenger assistance at the station, which means we get carried from the taxi to our train on a mechanised trolley that carries our luggage too.

Pigeons strut on the platform, pecking at dropped crumbs and imaginary titbits. Some, with stumps instead of clawed feet, waddle lopsidedly among the crowds and managing somehow to survive. Pigeons are great survivors. They can live anywhere – snowy mountain tops, deserts, forests and jungles, savannas, in cold and heat, drought and flood. Perhaps that's why the dove was the bird that showed Noah that the rains were over and why the dove is the emblem of peace. In the Second World War – or the First, I can't remember which – homing pigeons were used to send messages about troop movements and the enemy kept peregrine falcons to kill the messengers. Or it might have been the other way round. Our troops had the falcons and the enemy had the carrier pigeons.

I love crowds of people when I'm not getting crushed. I like car boot sales but not jumble sales. There's a middle-aged woman and a man in a trilby kissing by the sandwich stall. Very *Brief Encounter*.

We find our seats and settle Beelzebub's box on the floor under the table. We're going home! It's not the totally carefree, happy occasion I thought it would be. Daddy isn't here; Alistair isn't driving us. I am very sad about Precious. It's difficult feeling happy and sad at the same time.

At first I look out of the window at the factories and houses and back yards. I like back yards. A flock of white doves flutter like torn paper against the dark grey sky.

We play Scrabble and I win. Time rushes by, as do the chalk White Horse on a green hill, the canals, and ancient oak trees lonely in the middle of fields. The sun breaks through the clouds and sparkles in diamonds on the wide estuary of the Exe, where wading birds sift for food in the mud. My binoculars are packed, unfortunately.

'What do you want for your birthday, *Mutti*?'

'I have everything I could possibly want, my love. You, sweetheart, you and me and the pussycats, at home together.

And maybe a bottle of champagne with Alistair.'

'Not Daddy?'

'No, darling, sorry. Not Daddy. I think that part of my life is over.'

'But not for me. He's still my Daddy.'

'Sure he is. He'll always be your father. But not my husband.'

'I was horrid to Alistair.'

'Oh, he'll understand. Don't worry about it. Do something nice to make up for it, maybe?'

'What?'

'Oh I don't know. You'll think of something.'

We can still see the bones of the trees but some bushes are greening up, lovely pale green leaves uncurling. At Dawlish the railway runs right next to the sea and children stand on the red beach and wave as we go by and I wave back. There's an arch of rock in the sea and a tall thin rock standing on its own. We go slowly through tunnels. Twin black lambs run to their mother; a brown foal trots close by its mother's flank. There's a caravan in a field with a washing line attached to a tree where nappies flap in the breeze. We open up the packet of egg sandwiches that Mum made, and, as always, it smells like we've farted. And as always when I eat boiled eggs I see Paul Newman's stomach, swollen under the pressure of eating all those eggs in *The Hustler,* as he lies flat and his fellow prisoners push more whole eggs into his mouth.

I dip Willy's homemade ginger biscuits in my tea. Mum buys a small bottle of whisky from the buffet, drinks it and closes her eyes, her feet up on the empty seat next to her, her linen napkin, that she always takes on journeys on her chest. Beelzebub has slept for most of the journey. I open her box and get her out now and then to reassure her and give her water from a plastic cup. She gets her whiskers very wet. The ticket man strokes her and asks to see her ticket. I look horrified and he laughs. The woman with the food trolley asks if Beelzebub wants a saucer of milk but I say no thanks, she gets the squits if she drinks milk. Children stop to pet her, and women go 'Ah!' and she loves the attention, but tires of it suddenly and yawns, so I put her back inside the felt bag in the box.

Swans nest in long pale grasses. Stone hedges divide the little brown fields. Streams run alongside us. The sky is the colour of a dirty grey blanket.

The next carriage is packed with standing passengers and luggage in the aisle. There's a man with a bicycle in one of the lavatories and he won't let anyone in. We are in First Class, a necessity rather than a treat, said Mum, as we are both recuperating and need the extra comfort. Also, she doesn't want me to be exposed to viruses, so it's better if I don't mix with crowds if I can help it. I feel very grand. We get free bottled water, tea or coffee, fresh fruit and biscuits from the buffet but we have to show our tickets.

A man over the aisle holds a bald baby. A dummy wobbles in its moon face. His wife takes the dummy out and puts a spoon of something yellow in its mouth. The baby dribbles it all over her bib and giggles. She does it again. The mother shovels it back into her smiling mouth. Some of it goes down.

'Did Daddy hold me when I was a baby?'

'Not much, he was scared you would break.'

'Oh. Why did he think that?'

'Oh, he loved you so much, I think he felt helpless because he couldn't make you better.' Mummy looks away out of the window so I can't see her face. She is wearing dark glasses.

'My father was much more relaxed with you. He used to

throw you up in the air and catch you when you were about two. You loved it so. Do you remember?'

'No.'

I remember nothing of my babyhood, luckily. I was born with heart failure. I cried lots and didn't feed or thrive – an unhappy baby, I've been told. Not now, though. I am making up for it by being extremely cheerful. Perhaps I've cried all the tears I am supposed to have in this life. I lean up against Mum and rub my cheek on her arm. She puts an arm around me and squeezes. I'm not crying. I am *not* crying. It must be frustrating being a baby and not being able to tell people what's wrong with you. All you can do is scream.

I was born with major heart problems and there was no cure for what I had – Pulmonary Atresia, plus one or two other faults that enabled some of my blood to circulate. Having a new heart and lungs is not a cure, only treatment for last stage heart failure, but it is definitely an improvement on the quality of life I had before – not being able to walk across the room without feeling sick and breathless; chest infections every winter and if I caught a cold.

Large white clouds bubble up and bounce across a pale blue sky, robin egg blue. Poor Mr Robin, I feel so guilty about him. But maybe I wouldn't have found Beelzebub if the robin hadn't died. There's a blue gap between clouds that looks exactly like a Scottie dog.

I go back to reading Brett's book – *Hitchhiker's Guide to the Galaxy* – and realise it's a library book. I hope he has renewed it or he'll be in trouble when he takes it back. I lost two of Mum's books once – or rather I left them in a garden and they got soaked so I threw them away – it's a long story. Anyway, I ended up having to pay for them. I can't concentrate on Zaphod Beeblebrox, as Beelzebub is mewing. I think she wants to poo. Oh, dear, yes, she is pooing. Mum takes her to the lavatory and removes the soiled newspaper pages from the box and she settles down again. What a good little traveller she is – the kitten I mean.

I expect Douglas Adams got the name Beeblebrox from Beelzebub. They are so similar. Bubba has some water and a little kitten food and I sit her on my lap while she gives herself a good wash and brush up. At least her mother taught her to do that before she abandoned her. Poor motherless kitten, it makes me cry suddenly to think of the mother searching for her baby.

Oh dear, I'm having another of those emotional moments.

'Mum, have you noticed that Beelzebub's eyes have turned yellow?'

'Mmm.' She nods off again.

'*A book must be the axe which smashes the frozen sea within us.*' Franz Kafka said that. He was born in Prague, Czechoslovakia, and was Jewish. Willy told me that. I don't think that HGTTG does that exactly, but it makes me laugh out loud. It still hurts when I laugh, but it's worth it.

Thank goodness Mum isn't snoring; it's so embarrassing when she does that in public.

We are getting closer to home all the time. I put Bubba in her box, get up and walk as I haven't had any exercise today and I'm feeling a bit sore. I go to the buffet for bottled water.

The train manager says something unintelligible over the tannoy.

I'm so tired. I just want to be in my bed in the attic – will I be able to climb all those stairs? I haven't done much climbing up steps PT but I know it's going to be easier than it was BT.

I begin a poem about the hospital waiting room where I sat when Mum had her operation:

An ashtray full of ash and loss.
chairs sagging with too much sadness.

Then I started thinking about the waiting rooms at my transplant hospital.

Hospital Waiting Room

Two low tables
of scratched smoked glass
overthumbed magazines
and metal ashtrays
sour with an odour
of ash and loss.

We wait.
The chairs sigh for us.
They have absorbed
the sadness
of too many people.
They have had the stuffing
knocked out of them.

Emily Dickinson – who Mum loves – said: '*If I read a book and it makes my whole body so cold no fire can ever warm me, I know that is poetry. If I feel physically as if the top of my head were taken off, I know that is poetry.*'

Maybe one day I'll be able to write poetry that takes off the top of someone's head.

Cows and sheep fly past the window and the wind flings crows over the hedges.

I wonder if Mum would consider taking me somewhere

exciting when I am completely recovered – like Australia? Will I be allowed to fly? I'm not sure. Maybe the USA at least? Not for a year, I know, but after that? Perhaps not to somewhere like Malaysia or Indonesia because of tropical diseases, or Africa again, but somewhere hygienic like Switzerland would be good, except that I'm not keen on mountains or snow or fir trees.

How about Sweden? I could do a photo project on the Swedish film director Ingmar Bergman or visit the island where the writer and cartoonist Tove Jansson spent her childhood. I suppose when I start at school I'll have to stick to school holidays for going anywhere exciting. That was one advantage of being a child with health problems – Mum always took me somewhere tropical so we had winters in the sun. When I'm a famous photographer I will be able to go anywhere and make records of anything – buildings, animals, people, landscapes.

Brett might like me to travel with him to Australia to show me where he was born. In my dreams.

We've never been to America. Yes, New York should be top of my list of places to go. It will be like being in the middle of a movie. New York cabs – *Taxi;* The Empire State Building – *King Kong;* Grand Central Station – *North by Northwest;* Woody Allen's *Manhattan.* The entire city is a movie location. Daddy could come with us. Or if Mum doesn't want to go, Daddy could take me on my own. (Also, in my dreams.)

In the booklet they gave me at the hospital it says that heart and lung transplant patients are likely to have more than three years of life, possibly ten.

They don't really know, they've only been doing them for a few years. Let's be positive and assume I have ten more years. That means I'll live until I'm twenty-two. That's old. I ought to have a plan of action for things I must do. Perhaps one for each year. I must act wisely. It's a good reason not to put off dreams.

1. See New York.
2. Go to Australia and New Zealand, especially Wellington, the birthplace of one of my favourite writers, Katherine Mansfield.
3. Meet Nelson Mandela and go back to Africa.
4. Walk the West Cornwall coastal path or some of it.
5. Make sure Mum and Daddy are, if not together, then at least good friends and make sure he meets his Cornish family.
6. Read as many of the best books in the world as is possible. Start now!
7. Go on a course to learn about writing poetry (I suppose that should go before no. 4).
8. Be kissed by Brett.
9. Get married and have at least one child who will be healthy and whole and have a useful happy life. Maybe she'll be a world famous – an artist or writer, or maybe she'll be an ordinary, extraordinary person. (Maybe I shouldn't have any children as the world is already too full. I might adopt children with health problems.)
10. Visit the Galapagos Islands. I better do that before I have children as it's an expensive trip to make. Now I can't stop thinking about favourite things.

Things I love or have loved to do:
1. Sitting with my back to the wall on Porthmeor Beach watching the sun slipping into the sea.

2. Birding with Brett on Tresco.
3. Reading a favourite book. Better still, having a book read to me.
4. Playing Scrabble with Mum.
5. Watching old movies with Daddy.
6. Having Charlie on my lap.
7. Hanging out with Precious.
8. Laughing.
9. Watching the seagulls on the roof.
10. Playing with my kitten.

Favourite smells:
1. Cockle shells and mud at Old Leigh, Essex.
2. The air when you get out of the train at St Erth after being in London.
3. Second-hand book shops.
4. Charlie's fur.
5. Hot chocolate.
6. Daddy's aftershave (don't know what it's called – *Suave* or something).
7. *Moules marinière* and chips.
8. Sunburnt skin.
9. Horses' breath.
10. Primroses.
11. Leather car seats.

That's enough.

Favourite things to touch:
1. Cat's fur.
2. Daddy's hand in mine.
3. Grandpop's tattoos.
4. Mum's silk velvet dress.

5. Pebbles warming in my hand.
6. Books.
7. The wooden banister in our house at St Ives.
8. Mud under my toes.
9. Cold stainless steel.
10. A cool cotton pillow on my cheek.

Favourite tastes:
1. *Moules marinière* and chips.
2. Roast chicken and roast potatotoes with gravy and peas.
3. Coconut ice-cream.
4. Crumpets and strawberry jam.
5. Ginger biscuits dipped in tea.
6. Raspberries and cream.
7. Cornish clotted cream with meringue and strawberries.
8. Apple crumble and vanilla ice-cream.
9. Elderflower cordial.
10. Steamed samphire with melted butter and black pepper.

At least the last one makes me sound sophisticated.

Favourite sights:
1. A bluebell wood.
2. Starlings dancing together at dusk before going to roost.
3. Seagulls flying over the sea.
4. The first sight of St Ives through the gap in the wall by the coastguard cottages.
5. The sun setting into the sea at St Ives.
6. A field of daisies and buttercups.

Favourite sounds:
1. Charlie's 'hello' miaow.
2. Seagulls talking, crying, and all their sounds.
3. Starlings praying to the Sky God.
4. A robin's evening song.
5. The sea – whooshing and whispering, roaring and hissing, and when it sounds like an orchestra in the middle of the night.
6. Rain on the roof when I'm inside in the warm on a sofa wrapped in a woollen blanket.

I fall asleep and dream of Precious. We are running together along a warm sand beach. I wake with the shock of realisation that he is gone.

At Plymouth in one of the scruffy back yards next to the railway line there's a pink camellia bush standing alone. A game of football is played on bright green artificial grass at Devonport with artificial lighting. The teams look like robots or characters in an animated film.

Our train is trundling over the huge Isambard Kingdom Brunel bridge across the River Tamar into Cornwall. Swans are gliding by in front of the pub with the Union Jack painted on the front. Two herons stand sentinel on a gasholder, and Brent geese are heads down waddling through a field. Primroses grow in clumps on the railway banks, quite unreal-looking, like children's posies on a grassy grave.

I wish I had been able to go to Precious's funeral. I didn't get to say Goodbye. It was the same with Grandpop and Grandma. Then I was in hospital. Perhaps one day I'll be able to write a poem about him. I'll call it *When I Die*.

If I become a famous poet I might change my name. I have been known by various names:

Gorgeous Gussie (there was a tennis player with that nickname in the Fifties I think. She work frilly knickers).
Pansy. Don't ask why, I have no idea.
Honeybun – Daddy.
Gussiebun – Daddy.
Gussie – everyone.
Guss – everyone.
Sweetheart – Mum.
Sweetie-pie – Grandma and Grandpop.
Princess Augusta – Grandpop.
Org – Summer used to call me that and I hated it.
My Flower.

Why was I called Augusta anyway?
'Mum, why was I given my name?' She wakes and yawns.
'What?'
'Why did you call me Augusta?'
'Because you were born in August, and because it means sacred and majestic.'
'That's no reason.'
'It's a lovely name.'
'Hmm.'
'Unusual and memorable.'
'Hmm.'
The journey between Plymouth and St Erth is agonisingly slow. We stop at every station.
The rain hasn't stopped since Liskeard; drops run horizontally across the window and outside the world is grey and foggy.
I am so tired. Mum is too. I kick her when she snores.
The people with the bald baby must have got off when I

was asleep. We are the only people left in the carriage. Bubba is quiet. She must be so bored, stuck in the box, but I daren't let her roam.

Mum said she lost a kitten once on a long journey. She searched the train for it and thought it was lost forever. It had crawled over the top of the metal partition under her seat. Hours later it cried and she found it, but it wouldn't come out and she had to get the train manager to unscrew the partition to rescue it.

I'm too tired to be excited, and sad about so many things – Precious mostly. Mum has Agnes's address in West London and she'll write to her, if she's still there. What will she do? Will she wait for her daughters to arrive or will she go back to Zimbabwe to be with her husband?

I'm sad that I didn't achieve my aim to get Mum and Daddy together again.

And I'm ashamed I was horrid to Alistair. He can't help it if he isn't my father. I'll have to make it up to him. Perhaps I could get him tickets for a really important cricket match, except that that would be rather expensive. I know: I'll cook him and Mum a romantic dinner for two. No paper napkins, of course.

The sky is lightening as we reach Truro. Only half an hour before we reach St Erth. I go for a wee. The buffet is closed and the staff are relaxing, reading discarded newspapers. It must be strange to spend your working life on a train journey. I wonder if they suffer from land sickness when they get off?

'How's the little cat, then, my flower?' the manager asks.

'She's asleep.'

He must be Cornish, calling me 'my flower'.

I wake Mum and she goes to 'freshen up'. She looks better than she did when she first came out of hospital. I wonder if people will recognise me? I've put on a bit of weight, though I haven't grown upwards. And I'm pink – a real, normal pink.

We've gathered our bags on wheels and the kitten's box, which is very light, and when we get to Hayle we stand at the door, looking through the gap between the sand dunes at the estuary mouth. The town is like a white floating island against a grey-green, tumbling sea.

Mum opens the window.

The sun has come out into a broken patch of pale blue and the sweet smell of salt air takes my breath away. We draw slowly into St Erth station.

'Alistair!'

I jump into his arms and find myself crying on his tweedy shoulder as he hugs me.

I allow him to give Mum a big kiss and then grab his arm again.

'Alistair, I'm sorry I was rude to you on the phone. I love you, Alistair.' I reach up and kiss his cheek. He's smiling and hugs me to him again.

'Jeepers, you look well, Gussie,' he says.

'And who's this?'

He points at the box and Beelzebub stares out at him with yellow saucer eyes. He carries our bags over the step bridge. I practically skip up the steps. Oh, the clean smell of Cornwall! And there's a gull – two gulls – chatting above us, flying towards the town.

Mum looks so happy. So does Alistair. She gets in the front seat of his car; I am in the back with Bubba, suddenly wide awake.

There are spring flowers everywhere along the roadside – daffodils and narcissus and primroses, and three hens and a black cockerel peck at the grass verge by the farm at Lelant. We get to my favourite part – the gateway at the old coastguard cottages at Treloyhan, just beyond the big hotel. And there it is, my home, the little town, glowing white and gold, and I imagine I'm running along the sandy beach at Porthmeor, the surf booming as it does when the tide is low, my bare feet sinking into the warm sand, the late afternoon sun on my face and chest. Gulls skim the pink waves, rising and falling with the undulations, and I am running along the beach towards the sinking sun, my shadow tall behind me.

The Burying Beetle

Ann Kelley

ISBN 1 84282 099 0 PBK £9.99
ISBN 1 905222 08 4 PBK £6.99

The countryside is so much scarier than the city. It's all life or death here.

Meet Gussie. Twelve years old and settling into her new ramshackle home on a cliff top above St Ives, she has an irrepressible zest for life. She also has a life-threatening heart condition. But it's not in her nature to give up. Perhaps because she knows her time might be short, she values every passing moment, experiencing each day with humour and extraordinary courage.

Spirited and imaginative, Gussie has a passionate interest in everything around her and her vivid stream of thoughts and observations will draw you into a renewed sense of wonder.

Gussie's story of inspiration and hope is both heartwarming and heartrending. Once you've met her, you'll not forget her. And you'll never take life for granted again.

Gussie fairly fizzles with vitality, radiating fun and enjoyment into everything that comes her way. Her life may be predestined to be short but not short on wonder, glee, the love of things as they really are. It is rare to find such tragic circumstances written about without an ounce of self-pity. Rarer still to have the story of a circumscribed existence escaping its confines by sheer force of personality, zest for life.

MICHAEL BAYLEY

The Bower Bird
Ann Kelley
ISBN 1 906307 98 9
(children's fiction) PBK £6.99
ISBN 1 906307 45 8
(adult fiction) PBK £6.99

I had open-heart surgery last year, when I was eleven, and the healing process hasn't finished yet. I now have an amazing scar that cuts me in half almost, as if I have survived a shark attack.

Gussie is twelve years old, loves animals and wants to be a photographer when she grows up.

The only problem is that she might not live to grow up.

Gussie needs a heart and lung transplant, but the donor list is as long as her arm and she's not going to wait to get on with her life. She's got things to do now; tracking down her long-lost family, coping with her parents' divorce, and keeping an eye out for all the wildlife in her garden. And then there's Brett, the cute Australian boy with shockingly bad taste in girls...

Winner of the 2007 Costa Children's Book Award

It's a lovely book – lyrical, funny, full of wisdom. Gussie is such a dear – such a delight and a wonderful character, bright and sharp and strong, never to be pitied for an instant.
HELEN DUNMORE

An extract from The Burying Beetle

IT WAS AFTER I ate King that everything started to go wrong in our entire family, as if someone had put an evil spell onto us, a hex – like a bad fairy godmother had said at my birth, 'When you are eleven you are going to be struck by a sorrow so big it will be like a lightning bolt. There will be grief like a sharp rock in your throat.'

Silphidae – Necrophorus vespillo

The Burying Beetle has the curious habit of burying dead birds, mice, shrews, voles and other animals by digging the earth away beneath them. This accomplished, the beetle deposits her eggs upon the dead carcase, and when the larvae, or grubs, hatch they find an abundant food-supply near at hand. These insect-scavengers perform useful work, and it's largely because of their efforts that so few corpses of wild creatures are discovered. These carrion beetles also devour some of the decomposing flesh of the carcase, seeming to relish the bad odour that is given off. The Burying Beetle is rarely seen, unless close watch is kept over a dead rodent, bird, or other animal, and they seem to fly about on their scavenging expeditions in pairs, being attracted to the spot by scent. The commonest species is brownish black with bands and spots of orange-yellow.

British Insects by W. Percival Westell, FLS
(The Abbey Nature Books)

NOW, WHEN I throw out a dead mouse, I shall note where the body lands, watch for a pair of winged gravediggers to arrive and inhale as if they have just arrived at the seaside. I'll watch them tuck in to a morsel of meat, have sex on the putrefying flesh, then bury the evidence. Weird, or what!

Today, the eleventh day of August 1999, is my twelfth birthday.

The sun didn't rise this morning, or if it did it was so cloaked in dark grey cloud that the sky barely lightened. And then it rained. Not the sort of rain that looks like long knives, but a very Cornish drizzle – a sea mist, a mizzle that soaks you through just as thoroughly as a downpour.

We're staying in this cottage on the edge of a cliff overlooking a long white beach. Today, it's as if the cottage is in the sky on its own island of dull green, the tall pines hung with glistening cobwebs as if summer has gone and suddenly it's autumn. Like that feeling you get when it's time to go back to school after a long hot summer, and you put on your winter uniform for the first time, and can't remember how to tie the stupid tie, and you remember getting up in the dark, and going home in the dark. I hate that. The thought of a long dark winter ahead. But I do quite like the feeling of the season changing; my school beret snug on my head; knee-socks; lace-up shoes; the warm smell of my own breath under the striped woollen scarf.

Today, no birds come to the feeder hanging from the copper beech.

There's no sound of sea, even. A heavy grey blanket muffles the waves' collapsing sound on the sand. Ghost gulls moan and whine. There's not a hope in hell of seeing the eclipse, even though Totality is immediately over this part of Cornwall. But at 10.30am we put on waterproofs and walk through the gate onto the coast path. We push through sodden bracken, our shoes and jeans' hems soaked immediately, and walk to the railway bridge. All along the coast path there are little groups of people. A man with a small child on his shoulder. A family huddled under a golf umbrella. The sky a solid grey. No light bits, no fluffy bits or streaky bits, just a dead greyness, heavy with moisture. It's like being in the middle of a cloud. We *are* in the middle of a cloud.

People line the path at the highest point where there's a panoramic view of the bay and its beaches. Even the beach below us is crowded with people. Not loaded down with buckets and spades, ice creams, windbreaks, and with gritty sand in their private parts, but carrying umbrellas and wearing wellies and waterproofs. And we have all come together to share this moment. And just before 11am, as promised, we can see an even darker darkness spreading from the west over towards Clodgy, coming towards us, enveloping us in a cold clamminess. The gulls are silent.

And at the Moment of Totality, cameras flash on every beach on this side of the bay – Carbis, Porthminster, the Island, and over towards Newquay, Gwithian, Phillack, and Hayle. The sky is dark and all the bright stars have fallen and are twinkling among us.

Brilliant! Today at this very minute, I am twelve, and I feel in my bones that something momentous will happen to me. (Anyway, being eleven was so shitty, it's got to be better this year.)

The Blue Moon Book

Anne MacLeod

ISBN 1 84282 061 3 PBK £9.99

Love can leave you breathless, lost for words.

Jess Kavanagh knows. Doesn't know. 24 hours after meeting and falling for archaeologist and Pictish expert Michael Hurt she suffers a horrific accident that leaves her with aphasia and amnesia. No words. No memory of love. Michael travels south, unknowing. It is her estranged partner sports journalist Dan McKie, who is at the bedside when Jess finally regains consciousness. Dan, forced to review their shared past, is disconcerted by Jess's fear of him, by her loss of memory, loss of words.

Will their relationship survive this test? Should it survive? Will Michael find Jess again? In this absorbing contemporary novel, Anne MacLeod interweaves themes of language, love and loss in patterns as intricate, as haunting, as the Pictish Stones.

As a challenge to romantic fiction, the novel is a success; and as far as men and women's failure to communicate is concerned, it hits the mark. SCOTLAND ON SUNDAY

Me and Ma Gal

[B format edition]
Des Dillon

ISBN 1 84282 054 0 PBK £5.99

If you never had to get married an that I really think that me an Gal'd be pals for ever. That's not to say that we never fought.

Man we had some great fights so we did.

A story of boyhood friendship and irrepressible vitality told with the speed of trains and the understanding of the awkwardness, significance and fragility of that time. This is a day in the life of two boys as told by one of them, 'Derruck Danyul Riley'.

Dillon captures the essence of childhood and evokes memories of long summers with your best friend. He explores the themes of lost innocence, fear and death; writing with subtlety and empathy through the character of Derruck. This is a new edition from Luath Press.

Dillon's book is arguably one of the most frenetic and kinetic, living and breathing of all Scottish novels... The whole novel crackles with this verbal energy.
THE LIST 100 Best Scottish Books of All Time – 2005

Writing in the Sand

Angus Dunn

ISBN 1 905222 91 2 PBK £8.99

At the farthest end of the Dark Island lies the village of Cromness, where the normal round of domino matches, meetings of the Ladies' Guild and twice-daily netting of salmon continues as it always has done. But all is not well. Soon the characters are involved in a battle to either save or destroy the Dark Isle. But are they truly aware of the scale of events? And who will prevail?

It is a latter day baggy monster of a novel... a hallucinogenic soap... the humour at first has shades of Last of the Summer Wine, alternating with the Goons before going all out for the Monty Python meets James Bond, and don't-scrimp-on-the-turbo-charger method... You'll have gathered by now that this book is a grand read. It's an entertainment. It alternates between compassionate and skilful observations, elegantly expressed and rollercoaster abandonment to a mad narrative.

NORTHWORDS NOW

Undead on Arrival

Nick Smith

ISBN 1 905222 51 3 PBK £9.99

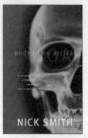

Glen Glass is living a tedious existence; bickering with his wife and resentful of his kids, until death hands him the opportunity to become the hero he never was.

Whilst re-evaluating his new-found freedom as a zombie, Glen inadvertently becomes involved in a plot worthy of one of his beloved spy movies. Battling his inherent idleness and the drawbacks of his new condition, he determines on finding the cause of his death, winning over the woman he loves and fighting against the forces which are increasingly endeavouring to restrict him and his kind.

This unique new novel from bestselling author Nick Smith (*Milk Treading, The Kitty Killer Cult*) is an eerie glimpse into a grave new world of corrupted morality, misbalance of nature and scientific experimentation. As compelling as it is original, *Undead on Arrival* challenges our attitudes towards life, death and everything in between.

My Epileptic Lurcher

Des Dillon
ISBN 1 906307 22 9 HBK £12.99

That's when I saw them. The paw prints. Halfway along the ceiling they went. Evidence of a dog that could defy gravity.

The incredible story of Bailey, the dog who walked on the ceiling; and Manny, the guy who got kicked out of Alcoholics Anonymous for swearing.

Manny Riley is newly married, with a puppy and a wee flat by the sea, and the BBC are on the verge of greenlighting one of his projects. Everything sounds perfect. But Manny has always been an anger management casualty, and the idyllic village life is turning out to be more *League of Gentlemen* than *The Good Life*. The BBC have decided his script needs totally rewritten, the locals are conducting a campaign against his dog, and the village policeman is on the side of the neds. As his marriage suffers under the strain of his constant rages, a strange connection begins to emerge between Manny's temper and the health of his beloved Lurcher.

The Underground City, a novel set in Scotland

Jules Verne
ISBN 1 842820 80 X PBK £7.99

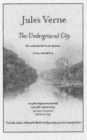

Ten years after manager James Starr left the Aberfoyle mine underneath Loch Katrine exhausted of coal, he receives an intriguing missive that suggests that the pit isn't barren after all. When Starr returns and discovers that there is indeed more coal to quarry, he and his workers are beset by strange events, hinting at a presence that does not wish to see them excavate the cavern further.

Could there be someone out to sabotage their work? Someone with a grudge against them? Or is something more menacing afoot, something supernatural that they cannot see or understand? When one of his miners falls in love with a young girl found abandoned down a mineshaft, their unknown assailant makes it clear that nothing will stop its efforts to shut down the mine, even if it means draining Loch Katrine itself!

Luath Press Limited

committed to publishing well written books worth reading

LUATH PRESS takes its name from Robert Burns, whose little collie Luath (*Gael.*, swift or nimble) tripped up Jean Armour at a wedding and gave him the chance to speak to the woman who was to be his wife and the abiding love of his life. Burns called one of the 'Twa Dogs' Luath after Cuchullin's hunting dog in Ossian's *Fingal*.
Luath Press was established in 1981 in the heart of
Burns country, and is now based a few steps up
the road from Burns' first lodgings on
Edinburgh's Royal Mile. Luath offers you
distinctive writing with a hint of
unexpected pleasures.
Most bookshops in the UK, the US, Canada,
Australia, New Zealand and parts of Europe,
either carry our books in stock or can order them
for you. To order direct from us, please send a £sterling
cheque, postal order, international money order or your
credit card details (number, address of cardholder and
expiry date) to us at the address below. Please add post
and packing as follows: UK – £1.00 per delivery address;
overseas surface mail – £2.50 per delivery address; overseas airmail
– £3.50 for the first book to each delivery address, plus £1.00 for each
additional book by airmail to the same address. If your order is a gift,
we will happily enclose your card or message at no extra charge.

Luath Press Limited
543/2 Castlehill
The Royal Mile
Edinburgh EH1 2ND
Scotland
Telephone: +44 (0)131 225 4326 (24 hours)
Fax: +44 (0)131 225 4324
email: sales@luath.co.uk
Website: www.luath.co.uk